ALEXANDREA LECHELLE
The Choices We Make
SOME LOVE STORIES DON'T END
THEY JUST DOUBLE BACK

I0769562

Acknowledgements

Dear reader,

Before we dive in, I just want to take a moment to say thank you.

To my beta readers—your feedback, encouragement, and time mean more than you know. Thank you for sitting with this story in its early stages and helping me polish it into something that feels true.

To those of you who read, rated, and reviewed *Loved By You*—your support filled my cup in ways I didn't expect. You helped me believe in myself as a writer, and you reminded me that stories matter. That Black love stories matter. And that there's room for mine.

This novella is a soft introduction to the *Double Back Diaries* universe. Not quite Book Two, but a prequel of sorts. A bridge between what was and what's coming. A glimpse at how far some of these characters have come—and how far they still have to go.

I hope this story wraps you up in something warm and familiar. And if it speaks to you, even just a little—please consider leaving a review. Your words matter more than you know.

With love and light,

Alexandrea Brumfield

Stay Connected

Love the vibes? Want more behind-the-scenes content, sneak peeks, exclusive bonus scenes, and writing updates before anyone else? Join my Patreon community for all that *and* more:

→ early access to new releases

→ character deep dives

→ writing sprints + livestreams

→ printable goodies

→ and a front-row seat to my indie author journey!

Subscribe at patreon.com/alexandrealechelle

(You know you wanna...)

And don't forget to follow me on social for daily updates, bookish chaos, and a whole lot of Black romance magic:

@alexandrealechelle on:

TikTok | Instagram | Pinterest | YouTube | Threads

Let's keep this story going—on the page *and* the timeline.

The Choices We Make

Official Playlist

Want to feel every moment of this story even deeper?
Press play and let the music guide you through the emotions, tension, and tenderness behind the pages.

Scan the code to listen on Spotify:

Headphones in. Heart open. Let's vibe.

Contents

Dedication

For those who knew the beginning mattered just as much as the ending.

For the friendships that turned into sisterhoods,

For the love that lingered before it ever had a name,

For the choices that echoed long before the vows.

This is where it all started.

This is the story behind the stories.

And I hope you feel every heartbeat of it.

Charisse

"Understanding" - Xscape

THE SCENT OF BURNT hair and Blue Magic filled the beauty salon as the sound of Toni Braxton's newest single thumped from the radio on the counter. Heat sizzled through the air as my stylist dragged a hot comb through the roots of the girl sitting in her chair. The girl flinched as the steam touched her scalp. Lisa sat under the dryer, flipping through an old Jet magazine, while Vivian was perched on the side, sipping a bottle of Evian, listening to me rant like she was getting paid.

"I'm done this time. For real." I leaned forward, tapping my acrylic nails on the Formica countertop. "That negro ain't got no damn sense, Vivian. I swear he sees a big booty and loses his mind."

Lisa let out a laugh and shook her head, flipping another page. "You say that every other month, Risse."

I cut my eyes at her but wasn't about to argue the truth. Still, this time felt different. "Nope. This ain't like before. This ain't some, 'I'll be back by Friday' type of thing. I packed my bags, and I meant it."

Too many times of me doing the laundry and finding little receipts and phone numbers in his pants pockets, faint traces of perfume and lipstick smudges along the collar of his work shirts. My man was treating his patients in more ways than one. Mr. Lewis Baptiste in the flesh. All I was missing was a sister to put a hex on him and make him faithful. But all I had was PJ. And I would not have my brother go to jail behind my foolishness.

Vivian took another sip, then sighed. Her voice was calm, like she was teaching a lesson. "Then why are you still talking about him?"

The question made me pause, but my stubbornness pushed through. "Because I'm pissed. Because I'm tired of being embarrassed." I sat in the chair next to Vivian, crossing my arms. "We can be out, having a good time, and all it takes is one heifer to walk by, and suddenly, I don't exist. He acts like he doesn't see me sitting right there."

Lisa smirked, finally pulling herself from under the dryer. "What did he do this time?" She asked, letting out a heavy breath.

I rolled my eyes so hard I saw the back of my head. "We were at the club last night because it's been so long since we've done anything together. Especially now that all his time is spent at the hospital. Well, this heifer comes galloping past our table, and I swear Kenneth's eyes stayed glued to her ass. He could've sniffed her ass crack from how hard he was staring." I sucked my teeth, the corner of my mouth curling after. "Then he wanted to pretend as if that's not what he was doing."

Lisa pressed her lips together, trying to hold back a grin, but Vivian just exhaled, shaking her head. Our stylist walked over, checking the roller set she'd given Lisa. "I tell you one thing. These so-called men these days ain't nothing but trash. They don't make them like they used to." She tapped Lisa on the shoulder, telling her she was ready for her to sit in her chair.

"You can say that again, Ms. Jean," I shouted across the open shop. A chorus of "mmhmm's" echoed my sentiments.

"Thank you, Ms. Jean. You've gotten her started now." Vivian dragged, continuing to sip on her water.

I walked over to the counter at the front, leaning back on my elbow, one hand on my hip. "And can you believe he had the audacity to say I was tripping?"

"Risse, you didn't even give him a chance to defend himself before you were freaking out at the table." Vivian crooked her head, exasperated with my retelling of events.

"Well, it doesn't matter because I'm done. I packed my stuff and I'm going home." I slumped against the counter, my mouth pouting as I looked at the floor. I glanced up to see Lisa staring at me with wide, green eyes, her mouth agape.

"Risse, you can't do that. Your life is here. Viv and I are here. What would we do without you?" Lisa sat back in the chair as Ms. Jean took out roller after roller.

Vivian, ever the poised one, studied me as she closed her water bottle, then asked, "Home? As in your Mama's house?"

I gave her a tight-lipped nod. "Yup. I'd rather be back in New Orleans, back in the projects, than feel like I'm competing with every woman with two legs."

Lisa sucked her teeth. "Girl, you run home again with your tail between your legs, Ms. Sonya's going to cuss your ass out."

"I know," I sighed, tilting my head back. I looked back at the shop floor, the once busy space now close to empty.

"Risse, I was there, and it wasn't as bad as you're making it seem," Vivian soothed, walking toward me. "Ms. Jean, please talk some sense into her."

"All I can say is if you let a man off easy once, he'll get off easy the next time." The hairdresser continued combing out Lisa's roller set, teasing her long, sandy-brown tresses into a pageant queen blowout.

Vivian wrapped an arm around my shoulder, holding me close. "Are you really done?" she asked me softly.

I hesitated, my fingers picking at a loose thread on the side of my jeans. "I don't know, Viv. I need it to be."

Lisa checked out her completed style in the mirror, then joined Vivian and me by the counter, crossing her arms over her chest. "Wants and needs are two different things, Risse."

Before I could respond, the shop door opened, letting the hot, sticky air of the late Houston summer spill inside. His cologne wafted through the air, citrusy and woody, making the freshly permed hair on the back of my neck curl. The room shifted, a slight pause in the conversation. It was as if the women in the shop were waiting to see the fireworks start.

Kenneth.

I turned to see him step inside, his gold chain glinting under the fluorescent lights, his fresh fade still sharp from the cut he got last week. So fine, and not all mine. His eyes locked with mine, his smirk cocky and amused, like he already knew how this was going to play out.

"Here we go," Lisa whispered in my ear.

"Hello, ladies," Kenneth said, stepping to the counter, his voice smooth as ever. "Risse, can I talk to you outside?"

I refused to answer him.

"Charisse," Ms. Jean started. "Go handle your business outside. I'll touch you up if I need to."

I looked over my shoulder at my hairdresser. She refused to meet my eyes. I let out a stream of air before walking around the counter, bypassing Kenneth's outstretched hand. I saw his head lower in exasperation as he followed me outside. I walked over to his car parked on the sidewalk, crossing my arms, tapping my foot against the cracked concrete. I was sure to angle my head so he'd know my time was short, so he'd better hurry and say what he had to say.

Instead, he laughed, leaning back on the hood of his car. "You done running yet?"

I stared him down, letting the weight of his question settle between us. "Running implies I'll be back. I ain't running, Kenneth. I'm leaving you. For good this time."

He chuckled slowly, shaking his head. "That's what you keep telling yourself?"

I squared my shoulders, my voice firm. "That's what it is. I refuse to let you keep making me feel less than. I'm done."

His tongue ran across the top row of his teeth. "You and I both know it's not that easy, Risse." He grabbed my arm, pulling me close. His thumb ran back and forth across my wrist, grazing the diamond tennis bracelet he'd gotten me after our last blow-up.

I looked into his eyes, scanning his face. If I weren't so pissed, I'd enjoy the smooth caramel complexion of his skin, the dark thick hair of his eyebrows and mustache. The way his eyes, piercing brown almonds, captured his prey. *Me.* I knew falling in love with him would be trouble. I saw the way girls fawned over him in college. It only intensified after he'd become a member of that black and gold. But he'd chosen me. *Me.* And now, I was paying the price. Countless times of those eyes wandering, followed by a licking of his lips. Dozens of nights of him coming in well past his hours, ending at the hospital.

"Risse, stop blowing things out of proportion. I was only trying to get the waitress's attention."

I jerked my arm away from him. "I bet you were. Then she'd be the next one calling the house, talking about 'Barbara, this is Shirley.' I'm tired of your shit, Kenneth. I packed my things, and I'm moving back home." I glared at him, daring him to change my mind.

Kenneth kissed his teeth, shifting his stance, glancing around everywhere but me. "Now, why do you want to go and do that? When you come back, all you'll do is complain about them and how they don't understand anything. You think I feel like hearing all that shit."

"Like I said before, you ain't gotta hear shit, because I'm not coming back." I placed my hands on my hips for emphasis as I stared up at him. His broad shoulders were tense, pulling the unbuttoned portion of his blue polo further apart.

He licked his lips, slipping his hand into the pockets of his starched jean shorts like he had all the time in the world. "Bet." He pushed off his car, jaw clenched, and walked over to the driver's side. He slammed the car door shut as he revved the engine.

Part of me wanted to beat the hood of his car for the way he'd dismissed me, but I had more class than that. *Or, at least I tried.* I turned and walked back into the salon, holding in the fury that burned in my chest. Vivian and Lisa gave me a once-over, their facial expressions mirroring each other. Worried.

"What did he say?" Lisa asked.

"He didn't even try to argue," I huffed, walking over to Ms. Jean's chair and sinking into the black vinyl. It clung to my skin when I made contact; my body heated from the humidity outside and my feelings toward Kenneth.

Vivian gave me a pointed look. "It's because he knows you're going to go back to him."

I swallowed, my stomach twisting, because that's what scared me most. What if they were right?

"See, that's what's wrong with y'all young things today." Ms. Jean looked at me through the mirror of her station. "Y'all don't know how to make a man beg, grovel, get down on his knees."

"Y'all don't understand," I muttered, mostly to myself.

Lisa raised an eyebrow. "Then help us understand."

I blew out a breath, focusing on Ms. Jean bringing the hot comb to the nape of my neck before smoothing the hair into the sleek French roll she'd done earlier. "It's not just about last night. It's every time. Every time I think we're getting somewhere, he goes and does some dumb shit like last night, making me question everything." I shook my head to keep the tears at bay. "I can't keep doing this."

Vivian walked over. "So, what's next then? You staying with your mama, back in the projects? You busted your ass to get out of there."

"I don't know. I just know I can't go back to that house. Not right now." I swiped at a tear escaping the corner of my eye. "I need to figure out what I want without him always in my face."

Vivian exchanged a look with Lisa. "And what if he doesn't let you?"

I shrugged. "Then that's his problem. Not mine."

Vivian took another slow sip of her water. "We'll see."

Vivian

"Another Sad Love Song" - Toni Braxton

THE WALLS OF GREENFIELD & Tate LLP were lined with portraits of men – white balding men to be exact – whose legacies loomed over every case, every closed-door conversation, and every opportunity that Black lawyers like myself had to fight for. But I was here, standing on the precipice of everything that was denied my ancestors and everything that would be afforded my children. A knot caught in my throat. I shook my head and looked around the room. Cigar smoke and overconfidence swirled around the room, though neither matched the suffocating feeling of having to prove yourself every single day.

I stood in the conference room, smoothing my navy-blue suit as I nodded along to the final words of my client's contract review. My mother's words echoed in my ear: *"Keep moving forward."* And, I had. Even though she was no longer here, I knew I made her proud with each accomplishment I made. I had spent the last three years building a reputation as a sharp, no-nonsense attorney, and I was so close to making partner that I could taste it.

But being close didn't mean a damn thing when the men I worked with always found a reason to move the goalpost.

"Excellent work, Mrs. Taylor," Mr. Whitemore, one of the senior partners, said as he stood, offering a handshake to our client. "You're in the best hands with Vivian here."

The words were meant to be praise, but I knew better than that. I had sat through too many meetings like this one to know my work was stellar. Yet, and still, once we were in front of the entire office, the credit landed in someone else's lap. Countless colleagues fumbled through cases only to be awarded promotions for which I'd never been considered. I had to be twice as good, twice as prepared, and twice as relentless.

"Thank you, Mr. Whitmore," I said smoothly, giving the client a firm handshake before gathering my files. I was supposed to stay late today, review more depositions, and have a few more meetings before attending another networking dinner where men shook hands over scotch while I fought to be acknowledged. But not today.

One of my good girlfriends needed me this weekend.

I was going home early and finally taking a day off.

"Mrs. Taylor," Whitmore called just as I reached my office door.

I turned, careful to keep my expression neutral. "Yes?"

He leaned against the conference table, arms crossed. "I heard you're missing the dinner later today."

I lifted my chin. "That's right. I have personal matters to attend to."

He raised an eyebrow, and I could already tell he was gearing up for one of his speeches to remind me that dedication was everything and that women in this field had to make certain "sacrifices."

"You know, the partnership committee is finalizing decisions in a few months. It's competitive."

"Of course."

"It's a pivotal time for you, Vivian." He pushed off the table, giving me a patronizing smile. "I'd hate for you to lose momentum. Peterson will be there."

I smiled back, steel beneath my composure. "I appreciate the advice, but I think my momentum is fine."

Before he could say anything else, I turned and walked out. By the time I reached my car, my hands were clenched around my briefcase. I let out a slow breath, trying to shake off the conversation.

Another month.

Another disappointment.

The pregnancy test sat on the bathroom counter, its single pink line glaring back at me like a cruel joke. My chest tightened as I gripped the edge of the sink, swallowing back the lump forming in my throat.

I barely heard Douglass enter until his hands settled on my shoulders. "Baby..."

I shook my head, willing my voice to stay even. "I don't want to talk about it."

He exhaled, resting his forehead against mine. "It's gonna happen, Viv. Our children will come when they're ready. When it's time."

I let out a humorless laugh. "And when is that, Douglass? Because every month, I feel like I'm failing."

His grip tightened just slightly. "You're not failing. You hear me." He turned me to face him, his dark eyes steady. "We're in this together. However it happens. Whenever it happens. It's going to be right."

I pressed my head against the firmness of his chest, letting the steady beat of his heart ground me. "I just hate feeling like I don't have control over this."

"Baby, what do you think it'll be like with a child?" He stared at me, his dark, round eyes lifting my spirits with every sweep of my face.

"Easy. You set the path for them, give them the tools and the access, and watch them achieve greatness. Look at us." I wanted my children to understand that greatness wasn't optional in this world – it was necessary. The moment you slowed down, the moment you took your foot off the gas, someone was there ready to count you out. I saw it happen with my mother. I was experiencing it now. But I'd be damned if my children ever had to fight this hard to be seen. I circled my arms around his waist, sinking further into his embrace.

He chuckled, tucking a piece of hair behind my ear. He pressed his lips to mine, delivering one of the sweetest kisses, taking my breath along with it. "Well, how about, for now, we control what we can. Take a break from all the stress. I have this big investment coming up.

You're up for junior partner at your law firm. Maybe this weekend away is exactly what you need."

I pulled back to look at him. "Yeah, maybe you're right. But I need you to promise me something."

He raised a thick eyebrow. "What?"

"Please don't tell Kenneth we're bringing Charisse back home. The last thing she needs is him showing up and trying to force a conversation she doesn't want to have. Especially not around her family. Her brother is crazy as hell."

"Vivi," he sighed, rubbing a hand over his jaw. "You know he's going to find out eventually."

"I know," I said, my voice firm. "But let her have these few days to breathe."

"Few days? She's been out of the house for the past week," he laughed, lifting me on the counter and placing his hands on either side of my hips. "How much space does she need to breathe?"

"Douglass," I pouted. "Try to understand. You know how your friend is. Almost makes me look at you sideways."

He studied me for a moment before nodding. "Alright. I won't say anything. I'll try talking some sense into him while y'all are away."

I let out a breath. "Thank you."

He tilted my chin up with his finger, giving me his easy, reassuring smile. "Now, are you ready for this trip?"

I nodded, even though I wasn't sure if I meant it.

⊷✦⊶

Walking into Lisa's apartment, it seemed as if Charisse had practically moved in over the past week. Her clothes were draped over the couch, her hair products crowding the bathroom sink, her heels stacked near the door like she lived there.

Lisa, ever the perfectionist, wasn't thrilled about it. "I let you crash for one night," she muttered, flipping through the mail. "One night, Risse."

Charisse stretched out on the couch, unbothered. "And now it's been a week. You love me, though."

Lisa shot her a flat look. "I tolerate you."

I laughed as I dropped onto the armchair, setting my purse on my lap. "You packed yet?"

Lisa let out a loud sigh. "Why am I even going?"

"Because I said so," I answered, giving her a pointed look.

Charisse smirked. "And because you know a good daiquiri and crawfish sounds nice right about now."

Lisa rolled her eyes. "You got a point. I could use a break from all these rice cakes and bland chicken I've been devouring, preparing for this wedding. One weekend won't hurt." Lisa drank a sip of coffee from the mug on the coffee table. "I know y'all got thoughts," she said, finally sinking into the plush couch. "So just go on and say them."

Charisse kicked her feet up on the coffee table, smirking. "Girl, you gonna marry Wesley?"

"It's not as simple as that," Lisa sighed.

"It kind of is," I shared, looking ahead at Lisa's TV. One of Bob Barker's Beauties was gracefully displaying one of the prize packages to the contestant on *The Price Is Right*.

Lisa shook her head, shifting uncomfortably. "Y'all know how this works. Our families are... connected. It's expected. It's always been expected."

Charisse scoffed. "Expected by who? Your parents? His? Them bougie-ass Black folks who throw charity galas and play tennis at the country club?"

Lisa shot her a look and then rolled her eyes. "Yes, Risse. All of the above."

"I get it," I said, tilting my head slightly.

Charisse turned to me, her eyes wide. "You get it?"

I exhaled and then met their gazes. "I'm not saying I agree with it, but I understand it. Black excellence isn't just about wealth. Legacy. Lisa's family, Wesley's family... They've been part of that world for generations. There's a sense of duty that comes with it. Risse, the way our lives are going, we'll be part of that same world. Kenneth's a doctor. You're a lawyer. Our kids are going to fall in love with people from this world, not how we came up."

"Exactly," Lisa shrugged. "It's not like I don't love Wesley. I do. He's a good man. Smart, successful, charming when he wants to be."

"But?" Charisse asked, arching a brow.

"But it's not... passion. It's not like that kind of love that sweeps you off your feet. It's comfortable. Secure."

Charisse rolled her eyes. "Sounds like settling."

Lisa snatched the magazine from Charisse's hands. "Sounds like stability."

I walked over, sandwiching Lisa between Charisse and me on the couch. "Lisa, are you sure that's what you want?"

"I don't know," she said, sinking back. "Maybe."

"If you gotta think that hard, then it ain't it," Charisse scoffed.

Lisa gave her an annoyed look. "Not everybody wants a love that burns that house down, Charisse."

"First of all, it was a shirt. And, in my defense, it had a lipstick stain on the collar. And two, not everybody wants a love that feels like a business merger either," Charisse countered. "Look, I get it. Your family's got money, his family's got money, and y'all are supposed to create some kind of damn dynasty. But what happens when you wake up one day and realize money and status ain't enough?"

Lisa shook her head, exasperated with the conversation we'd had at least two times before today. "It's not just about me, though. This is about legacy, about continuing what my parents built."

"That's the hard part, isn't it? Carrying the weight of what our families expect of us."

Lisa glanced at me, squeezing my hand. "You feel it, don't you?"

"In a different way, but, yes, I do. Our ancestors toiled the land. We're building the foundation for our children to thrive. It's tough as hell."

Charisse waved us both off. "It's the truth, but y'all make it sound exhausting." She ran a hand over Lisa's back. "You think Wesley's on the same page?"

Lisa hesitated. "I think Wesley...understands. We both know what's expected, and we've found camaraderie in that."

Charisse blew a stream of air from her mouth. "That is going to be one boring marriage. It's okay, though. I'm sure I'll have plenty of entertainment to share."

Lisa stood, throwing a few of Charisse's clothes on the floor. I looked on as my two good girlfriends pestered each other. I'd met them both in college, as we'd been assigned roommates. From the moment I met Lisa, I knew she came from money. It oozed from the designer suitcases she brought in with her, contrasting with the basic suitcase I had and Charisse's worn duffel bags. Regardless of our different upbringings, in that first semester, we'd grown to be thick as thieves.

Lisa clipped up her hair as she and Charisse continued to go at it, taking light jabs at each other. I tuned them out, settling into Lisa's couch, my head resting on the back. My thoughts drifted back to Douglass. To everything we'd been trying to build. Everything that felt just out of reach.

"Viv," Charisse yelled, breaking me out of my spell. "What's wrong with you?"

"Nothing, girl," I said without hesitation. "Just trying to take a cat nap while I wait on the two of you."

"Nope," Charise said, eyeing me up, her eyes laser-focused on me. "Lisa and I have been sharing all our business. Now is not the time for you to keep yours to yourself."

Lisa walked up next to Charisse, their bantering ceasing to gang up on me. "Spill it, Viv. We know it's not relationship issues."

"No," I sighed. "No offense, but listening to the two of you makes me grateful every day that I have Doug. I'm just tired, that's all. You know how hectic it's been at the firm and with everything else. I'm just ready for things to fall into place." I broke free from the investigative gazes to tune into the participants coming down the stage.

Lisa and Charisse looked at each other, conversing with their minds. "Fine. But you know we're both here when you need us. Right?"

"Yes," I laughed. "I know. I promise I'm just tired. I'm good."

"You're not, but we'll let you live for now. We know you'll come around when you're ready," Charisse smirked, going back to packing her bags. They knew what I was going through and respected my decision not to speak about it.

And for that, I loved them even more.

When they turned to finish their packing and bickering, I rubbed a hand over my stomach, swallowing the lump in my throat. Maybe this trip was exactly what I needed. A few days away from work. Away from trying to make something happen that just wouldn't. Just me and my girls.

Maybe, for once, I needed to just let go.

I glanced up at the ceiling, exhaling softly.

Relaxing.

If only it were that easy.

Lisa

"What About Your Friends" - TLC

B Y THE TIME WE crossed the New Orleans-Metairie border, the sun had dipped below the skyline, casting an amber glow over the city. The air was thick and humid in that way that stuck to your skin, but the smell, the mix of spicy seafood, damp pavement, and a hint of the Mississippi River, tickled my breath.

Charisse gripped the wheel, her knuckles tight against the wood grain wheel, her eyes locked on the road like she was holding back everything that had been boiling in her since we left Houston. Vivian sat quietly in the backseat, staring out the window, lost in whatever thoughts she wasn't sharing with us. And me? I just wanted a damn drink and food with enough butter to fill a churn.

Not because the drive was long, but because the closer the days got to my wedding to Wesley Wright, heir to the Wright Horizons Real Estate throne, the heavier my thoughts felt. The looming deadline of forever. This was supposed to be my fairytale wedding. I was about to marry a man who checked all the right boxes but didn't check the one that mattered most, the one that made me feel something real. I was supposed to be excited, head over heels.

But all I felt was trapped.

I stretched, arching my back before glancing at the dashboard. "First stop, somewhere with good food. I'm starving."

"You're always starving," Charisse huffed but smirked. "That's what you get for eating like a bird these past few months."

"Oh, please. Anybody would be starving after that long ass drive," I shot back. "You not?"

She sighed, her shoulders easing just a bit. "Mama probably cooked. You know she always got something ready."

Vivian spoke, her voice softer than usual. "That woman stays feeding people."

I glanced at her through the rearview mirror. She hadn't said much the entire trip, but something about her was heavy. I wanted to ask, but I knew Vivian. She'd talk when she was ready.

"Okay, serious question," I said, turning down the volume as TLC continued to sing about friendship in the background. "What's your mama going to say when we show up on her porch?"

Charisse shook her head, her bangs sweeping across her eyebrows. "Nothing. My mama loves it when I come home. I'm the favorite child."

I looked back at Vivian, her round brown eyes matching my disbelief.

"Risse, your mama's going to cuss your ass out," I laughed. "Then, she'll cuss us out for going along with you. Is your brother going to be home?"

"Probably," she shrugged. "You know his ass can't stay out of the projects. That's why I'm the favorite. I'm the one who made something of myself."

"And yet, you're still trying to move back home?" Vivian asked Charisse. She shot daggers at her through the rearview mirror.

"How about you hush up and go back to sleep since you're so tired?" Charisse scoffed, turning the volume back up.

Charisse turned onto Orleans Avenue, and just like that, we were pulling up to her mother's unit in the Lafitte projects. The moment we pulled up, the front door swung open, and Ms. Sonya stepped onto the small concrete porch, arms folded, lips pursed. She looked like she'd been waiting all day just to fuss.

"Well, well, well. Look who the hell decided to come home," she called out, her voice carrying across the street. She was a sturdy woman, pecan-brown skin covering big bones. The scowl gracing her face would scare even the toughest of men.

Charisse sighed as she cut the engine. "Here we go."

We climbed out of the car, the sticky night air wrapping around us as we grabbed our bags. Before we even got to the steps, Ms. Sonya had her hands on her hips, scanning Charisse from head to toe like she was looking for evidence of bad decisions.

"You ain't call, you ain't write, you just show up."

"Mama, please," Charisse groaned, rolling her eyes. "Can I get in the house first?"

Ms. Sonya squinted but stepped aside, letting us pass. "Go on, then. But you know I got words for you."

Inside, the house smelled like fried fish and lemon-scented cleaner. The living room looked exactly as I remembered. Plastic-covered couches, an old wooden coffee table stacked with Jet and Essence magazines, a fresh bouquet of lilies, and a box fan humming in the corner. It wasn't anything like the custom-made couches and drapes I was used to growing up, but it felt like home all the same.

I flopped onto the couch, running a hand through my long, pressed-out tresses. "Whew. Felt like a damn road trip."

"Because it was," Vivian muttered, sitting beside me.

Ms. Sonya sat in the armchair across from us as Charisse went to the kitchen. She eyed Vivian and me up and down, not missing a thing. Her sharp gaze cut right through the silence like a knife. "You lookin' too skinny, Vivian. Y'all been feeding this girl?"

"It's just stress, Ms. Sonya. I'm up for junior partner at my law firm," Vivian smiled.

"Ummhuh," Ms. Sonya smirked. "And what about you, Miss Thang?" she asked me. "You getting cold feet yet? You look just as 'stressed' as Vivian."

The question caught me off guard, and my stomach twisted. "What?"

She gave me a knowing look, raising one eyebrow. "You about to walk down that aisle. Are you sure you're ready?"

"Ms. Sonya," I started, my pageant queen instincts kicking in. "Planning the wedding of the year is quite stressful."

"Mmhmm. That's what women say when they ain't sure," Ms. Sonya responded, shaking her head. "Shit, at least you making moves to jump the broom, unlike this silly girl of mine."

I opened my mouth, but nothing came out. Because she wasn't wrong. She'd read me like an open book exam. I felt exposed like she saw right through the performance I'd been putting on for everyone, including myself.

Ms. Sonya left Vivian and me sitting in stunned silence after her targeted comments, disappearing into the kitchen. Vivian looked at me carefully, like she wanted to say something but didn't. A few minutes later, Ms. Sonya returned with two plates of red beans, rice, and fried catfish, setting them down in front of us. "Eat."

Charisse came out behind her with a plate of her own. "Mmm. Mama, I've been missing your cooking, something bad."

"Wouldn't have to miss it if you came around more often. Y'all thirsty?" Ms. Sonya asked, still standing. "I just put some cold drinks in the icebox, but I got a little Tang left."

"Mama, sit down. You act like Viv and Lisa never been here before." Charisse continued to shovel mouthfuls of the seasoned red beans into her mouth, stopping now and then to suck on the pork bones Ms. Sonya used to give the dish extra flavor.

"That's what it feels like. It's been how long since y'all asses came out this way?" Ms. Sonya sat back down in the armchair, turning to glare at her daughter. "And, I know this ain't no damn visit 'cause you missed my red beans. What the hell Kenneth done did now?"

Charisse rolled her eyes, placing her plate on the coffee table in the middle of the room. Vivian and I continued eating, choosing to watch the showdown between Charisse and her mother.

"Mama, why is it so hard for you to believe I came home because I missed you?"

"You ain't been home, 'cause you 'missed me,' since you left this house for college. So what did he do this time? And how long you gon' be here 'til you run back?"

Charisse stood, staring her mother down. I never dared to talk back to my parents. They ran our house with an iron fist. There wasn't a move I made without my parents telling me what it would be. On the other hand, Charisse and her mother were the same: mouth, body, and all. It was as if Ms. Sonya had spit out her carbon copy.

"You know, if you want to do me like this, we can stay at a hotel."

Ms. Sonya smacked her lips and waved her daughter's words off. "Girl, sit your narrow-ass down and finish eating. You crazy if think I'm 'bout to have my baby girl staying at some damn hotel."

Charisse smirked as she grabbed her plate, sitting back down to finish her food. Ms. Sonya turned on the TV to fill the silence.

Later that night, we sat on the front porch, drinking wine coolers, watching the community move like it always had. Across the courtyard, a group of kids played under the glow of the streetlights, their laughter mixing with the faint sounds of bass-heavy music blasting from a stereo somewhere in the distance.

Charisse stretched her legs out, resting her feet on the porch railing. "It feels different being back."

I took a sip of the sugary alcoholic drink. "Different how?"

Charisse shrugged. "Like...I don't know. Like I left something unfinished."

Vivian shifted beside me, playing with the edge of her cup. "Maybe you did."

Charisse nudged Vivian. "You ready to tell us what's going on?"

She forced a smile. "I'm fine. Just thinking."

"About?" I asked, turning toward her.

She hesitated, then shrugged. "Everything. Nothing."

Charisse gave her a look but didn't push. "Well, stop thinking so hard. We're here to relax."

Ms. Sonya's words echoed in my mind, but I kept them to myself. Because the truth was, we all had something left unfinished. Charisse had Kenneth. Vivian had the pressure of completing the final task on her perfect life checklist. And me? I had a wedding dress waiting for me back in Houston and a question sitting heavy on my chest.

Was I ready for forever?

That was the thing about home. No matter how far you ran, it always had a way of pulling you right back into everything you thought you escaped. And whether Charisse was ready to admit it or not, we all knew this wasn't just about a visit.

This was about Kenneth.

And sooner or later, she was going to have to face him.

Just like I was going to have to face myself.

My pager on my hip beeped. I pulled it off my waistband and squinted. *Mama.* I hopped up and made my way inside the house, knowing I'd receive about five more pages if I didn't call my mother back right away.

"Ms. Sonya, can I use your phone to call my mother? I'll cover the long-distance fees. You know I'm good for it."

Ms. Sonya nodded her head but pushed the phone toward me anyway. "I see she not playing around still, huh?"

"That's an understatement," I replied, dialing my mother's number.

When she answered, I couldn't get a word out before her sharp voice cut through the receiver. "Lisa Marie! Where are you? I paged you twice!"

I hesitated, then answered. "Hey, Mama. I'm in New Orleans, visiting Charisse's mama. You remember Ms. Sonya, don't you?"

"Don't *hey mama* me," she said, her voice clipped but warm. "Did you forget you had a wedding to plan?"

I forced a chuckle. "I didn't forget."

"You sure? Because you still haven't sent me the final guest list. And your dress fitting. Don't think I don't know you canceled last week."

My grip on the cup in my hand tightened. "I've been busy, Mama."

My mother sighed. "Lisa, baby. I just want to make sure everything is in place. This is going to be the wedding of the decade, let alone the year."

My throat tightened. I swallowed hard, forcing my voice to sound light. "I know, Mama. It's exciting."

She let out a relieved sigh. "Good. Because this is the rest of your life. These are the choices we make. And I just want the best for you."

I nodded, even though she couldn't see me. "I know, Mama. Let me go. Viv and I are with Risse, visiting her mom."

"Alright. Don't indulge too much. I'm going to get another dress fitting on the books for this week."

"Okay, Mama." I ended the call and stared at my screen, my chest feeling tight.

When I turned around, I jumped and threw a hand to my chest. Ms. Sonya stared at me with her piercing almond eyes, her lips curled just so, a hand on her hip. "You surely do seem excited about this wedding," she announced before walking to the back of her home.

I barely had a chance to steady my nerves when my beeper went off again. I exhaled, already dreading another page from my mother, but when I checked the screen, my breath caught in my throat. *Trent.*

I glanced at the front porch and the back of the house before pulling the corded phone into the hallway bathroom. I dialed the number, tapping my fingers on the sink counter as I waited.

Two rings in, he picked up. "Hey, Lisa."

"Trent, why are you paging me? I told you I was busy this weekend," I murmured, my voice low.

"You know I got my ways," he chuckled.

I smiled, twirling the cord between my fingers. "What do you want?"

"You in New Orleans?"

I rolled my eyes. "Yeah. How'd you figure that out?"

"That 504 popped up on my caller ID," he laughed.

"Well, it's supposed to be a secret, so don't go blabbing your mouth to Kenneth. My girl needs a break to clear her head."

"Nah, they gonna figure they shit out. I want to talk about us." My stomach flipped, even though I knew it shouldn't.

"Trent, there is no us. I told you I'm getting married."

"So, when should we see each other?"

I exhaled. "That's not a good idea."

Trent's voice dipped, teasing. "Was it a good idea you called me back?"

"Bye, Trent," I snapped, hanging up the phone. When I stepped into the hallway, Vivian and Chaisse were walking back inside.

"Lisa, why you got the phone in the restroom?" Charisse asked, going toward the fridge.

"She was talking to her mama," Ms. Sonya replied, coming back to the front. "Course, I don't know what kind of conversations people have with they mama where they have to hide in the restroom. But hey, at least she calls her mama."

"Alright, Mama. I get it." Charisse grabbed a few more wine coolers from the fridge and shrugged for Vivian and me to follow her back outside. We spent the rest of the night reminiscing about our college years and throwing back drinks. Wine coolers turned into shots of Ms. Sonya's Seagram Seven, or "Seven Sisters" as she liked to call it.

My mother's words reverberated in my head all night.

The rest of my life.

I'd spent the last few weeks convincing everyone around me I was ready to tie the knot to someone I had no passion for. I glanced at my friends, but neither of them said a word about the wedding all night. Because we all knew. I didn't sound sure.

Because I wasn't.

Kenneth

"Please Don't Go" - Boyz II Men

T HE COLD BITTERNESS OF the beer coated my tongue before I swallowed it down. I took another slow sip, setting the bottle on the table in front of me. The bar was dim, the kind of place that smelled like decades of spilled whiskey, fried chicken wings, and worn leather. A couple of old heads were perched at the far end, talking about the NBA playoffs over brown liquor, while the faint hum of Al Green drifted from the jukebox in the corner.

Across from me, Douglass stretched back in his chair, eyeing me with amusement in his eyes. His gold wedding band caught the light as he lazily turned the bottle. To his right, Trent, the ever-smug financial analyst, leaned forward like he had me all figured out.

"Man, you're letting her run you ragged like this?" Trent finally asked, shaking his head. "I mean, damn, Ken, you look stressed."

I scoffed, forcing a smirk. "Ain't nobody running me ragged. Risse just wants to play games. She does this every few months. Packs up.

Makes a big fuss. I let her get her little tantrum out, then she brings her ass right back."

Douglass let out a low chuckle, tilting his bottle. "Ain't no woman packing up and leaving over nothing, man."

My jaw was tense. How was it that Charisse walked out on us, yet I was facing persecution? "Man, y'all don't even know Risse like that."

Trent lifted a hand in mock surrender. "I know women. And if she's gone, it's because you let her think she could leave. Where she at, anyway?"

Douglass rubbed his chin as he looked around the bar. *Oh, his ass knew something.*

"Say, Doug. You over there looking like Stevie Wonder. You got something to share with the table?"

Douglass shook his head, finishing his beer. "I don't have anything to say."

I smacked my lips. "Doug, you over here sleeping with the enemy. I know you know where my woman is." Douglass made a motion, zipping his lips.

"That's cold-blooded, bruh," Trent laughed. "We're supposed to be brothers, and you're keeping secrets?"

"Even if I did know where she was," Doug started, leaning forward. "What were you going to do? Smack her over the head with a club and drag her back to Houston?"

"Her ass left Houston," I half asked, half yelled. The old heads at the bar looked over their shoulder, laughing at my outburst.

"Damn, man," Trent laughed. "Shit must be bad if she left the state." Douglass cut his eyes at Trent. "Shit, my bad."

"She went back to her mama, huh?" Douglass and Trent refused to meet my eyes. Douglass picked this moment to flag the waitress down for another round of beers. "Hell yeah, she went back home."

"So, she went back home, around her people, around her brother that always got something sick to say about you, and you sitting here drinking a beer? Not doing a damn thing about it?" Trent shrugged off.

I flexed my hands, relaxing back in my chair. "What do you expect me to do? Show up with flowers and a love song? Hit a dance number in the rain?"

Douglass chuckled. "You could give her some space, let her figure out her feelings, instead of trying to force her back. Then, stop acting stupid. Otherwise, I'm going to have to stop claiming you. I don't want my wife looking at me crazy."

"And you need to hurry up before somebody else comes to take her from you," Trent smirked.

"Ain't nobody taking my woman," I huffed. "Charisse got a temper, but she ain't dumb."

"I bet that's exactly what she's telling herself right now about you."

I leaned back, stretching my arms across the table. "Y'all funny. Ain't nobody replacing me."

Douglass sipped his fresh beer, leveling me with a look. "Then why do you look like you already know you're losing?"

I pressed my lips into a tight line. I didn't like how Douglass always saw through me. Didn't like the way Trent's words burrowed under my skin. Didn't like how, despite all my confidence, there was a nagging feeling deep down in my chest that Charisse might be done this time.

I couldn't admit it, not out loud, but something about this time felt different. The way she left, the way she didn't look back as I drove off after leaving her on the curb at her hair salon. She packed up and ran home to the people who never thought I was good enough for her to begin with. Who wouldn't want their daughter to be with a doctor? I spent years trying to prove them wrong, to no avail. But what if they were right?

"She's being dramatic, " I said, more to convince myself than anyone else. "She's just mad about that night at the club. She'll cool off."

Trent raised an eyebrow. "You sure?"

I couldn't give him a sure answer. I just took another long pull from my beer, letting the silence hang between us.

After a moment, Douglass leaned forward, resting his arms on the table. "Look, man. You know how Charisse is. She needs to feel like you give a damn. Not just because you don't want to lose her, but because you care."

I exhaled sharply, running a hand over my face. "Man, y'all act like I don't love this woman."

"We know you do," Douglass said. "But does she?"

I sat still, the weight of the question settling over me. I knew how to make Charisse laugh, knew where to kiss her to make her melt, and knew every little thing that made her tick. But did she know, really know, how much she meant to me?

My fingers drummed against the table. "She'll see."

Trent laughed. "See what? That you're stubborn as hell."

My smirk returned, but it didn't quite reach my eyes. "Nope. That she's mine. Always has been. Always will be."

Douglass tilted his head, narrowing his eyes. "Kenneth."

Something about the way Douglass said my name made me tense. He was warning me, but I ignored him. I wasn't just some man chasing his girl. This wasn't just about some off-and-on-again relationship.

Charisse wasn't just my woman.

She was my world.

My life.

I swallowed, gripping my beer tighter. The truth of us settled deep in my gut. We made a promise to each other. And now, she was back home, running from that promise. Running from me.

And I didn't know how to stop her.

"She's just mad," I said again, but this time, my voice lacked conviction.

Douglass sighed, leaning back. "If you believe that, you wouldn't be sitting here drinking with us. You'd be getting your woman back."

I stared at my friends, my brothers, who sat there, smirking like they'd already seen the whole thing play out. Maybe they had. Maybe they all knew something I didn't want to admit yet.

That maybe, this time, Charisse wasn't coming back.

My jaw clenched. *No.* That wasn't happening.

I pushed up from the table, finishing the rest of my beer in one gulp before slamming the empty bottle on the table. "Y'all busy this weekend? I need y'all's help with something."

Trent laughed, shaking his head. "Long as I'm back by Sunday night, I'm good."

I looked over to Douglass.

"Viv is going to kill me," he grimaced. "When she kicks me out, just know I'm crashing at your place," he added, pointing at me.

I didn't say anything as I turned for the door, my heart thumping in my chest. I wasn't worried.

Charisse would come back.

She always did.

Charisse

"My Lovin' (You're Never Gonna Get It)" - En Vogue

NEW ORLEANS HAD A pulse that I could feel deep in my chest. The city never slept, and neither did my thoughts. The moment my eyes opened to the dim light seeping through the blinds of my childhood bedroom, I felt it. That knowing, that tension pressing against my ribcage like a warning.

Kenneth was coming.

I could feel it in my bones, the same way I could sense a storm rolling in before the first drop of rain hit the pavement. It was only a matter of time before he found out I was home. Before he came, stomping through the Lafitte, trying to play savior in a situation he'd caused in the first place.

Not this time.

I stretched my arms over my head, the scent of fried bacon and butter hitting my nose as I swung my legs out of bed. Mama had been up cooking, which meant I had approximately five minutes before she started asking me about Kenneth. I wasn't ready for that conversation.

Not yet.

I pulled on a pair of high-waisted denim shorts, rolled at the hem, and put on a tank top before heading out of my room, my bare feet silent on the floor. Vivian was already at the kitchen table, her hands wrapped around a coffee mug, looking lost in her thoughts.

"Morning," I mumbled, sliding into the chair across from her.

Mama turned from the stove, raising an eyebrow. "You sleep okay?"

"Yeah," I lied.

She hummed, her way of letting me know she didn't believe a damn word I just said. "I made some grits. Added a little pinch of sugar to yours."

I grabbed the bowl without hesitation, blowing the piping hot meal to cool it down. "Thanks, Mama. Where's PJ?"

"Somewhere running the streets. You know you gon' have to answer to him if he catches you here."

My brother swore he ran my mother and me. I couldn't understand why he thought he had some power over me when he dedicated his life to the streets, doing God knows what. Don't get me wrong, I love my brother, I just hate the life he chose for himself. How was it that two people raised in the same house could turn out so differently?

"If PJ comes around, I'm sure he'll be more than happy to see me, unlike the warm reception you gave."

She nodded but didn't move, her sharp eyes scanning me like she was reading every single thought running through my head. "What y'all got planned for the weekend? I know not to stay inside all day. It's a block party later today."

I chewed slowly, trying to play it cool. "I don't know yet."

"Mmmhmm." She wiped her hands on a dish towel and leaned against the counter. "Well, I hope you ain't thinking you can hide in here forever."

Vivian coughed, barely masking her laugh. I shot her a look before turning back to Mama. "Who said I was hiding?"

Mama gave me a knowing smile and picked up her coffee. "Ain't nobody said it. I just know you, baby girl. And I know when Kenneth bring his ass on my porch step, you gon' have to face him sooner or later."

I rolled my eyes, discarding the beignet I'd started. "I'm going wake up sleeping beauty."

Vivian watched me as I started to leave the kitchen. "Oh, you're just mad because she's right," she shouted behind me.

My girls and I ended up on Claiborne Avenue, the familiar streets buzzing with life as I drove past corner stores and fruit vendors. The air was thick with the smell of hot sausage and boiling crawfish, and for a brief moment, I let the nostalgia settle in my bones.

"I'm about to run into the store. Y'all want anything?" I asked Vivian and Lisa, parking on the sidewalk next to the Circle Food Store.

"Ooh. Get me one of those hot sausage po-boys," Lisa chimed, digging into her purse for cash. "If my mother's going to pester me about going to the gym every day when we get home, I'm going to make it worth it."

"Viv, you want something?" I asked, looking back.

She turned her head from the car window as if she were caught. "Oh, no," she said nervously. She took a quick scan around the building before she spoke again. You know what? You can get me one of those fried hand pies—cherry. Oh, and a shrimp po-boy—fully dressed. And see if they have a pineapple Big Shot."

"Damn, Viv. This the corner store, not the grocery store," I smirked, getting out of the car. I walked into the store, speaking to the cashier before perusing the aisles. After grabbing a bag of CheeWees, Viv's pie and drink, I stood in line to place her and Lisa's order.

Then, I heard him.

"You thought I wasn't going to find you?"

I didn't have to turn around to know it was Kenneth. His voice carried that mix of arrogance and amusement that always made me want to kiss him and slap him at the same time. I exhaled slowly before facing him. He looked the same, too fine for his own good, standing there in a crisp white tank and fresh sneakers, his gold chain glinting against his caramel skin.

"I wasn't hiding," I said, lifting my chin.

Kenneth smirked, stepping closer, his breath tickling the back of my neck. I closed my eyes and took a breath, steadying my nerves.

"Oh, so you just forgot to mention to your husband that you were leaving the state?"

I moved forward, refusing to let him pull me into his orbit. "Ex-husband. As soon as I get back to Houston, I'm filing for an annulment."

I looked over my shoulder, seeing the tension set in his jaw. I smirked and rolled my eyes as I greeted the cashier. "Can I get a hot sausage po-boy and shrimp po-boy, fully dressed?"

"Talk to me, Risse."

"I knew Vivian wouldn't be able to hold water," I said to no one in particular, rolling my eyes and moving to the side. He followed close behind me. "I'm not doing this here, Kenneth."

Kenneth tilted his head. "Where you want to do it then? Because I'm not leaving until we talk."

I ignored him, grabbing the food I thought about throwing away for the betrayal my so-called friends did. When I went to pay, Kenneth pushed my hand to the side, shoving a plastic card toward the man behind the counter. "I'm not about to have my wife pay for something when I'm standing right here."

There it was.

This all-encompassing claim he made on me. Always announcing to the world that I was his and no one else's. But when it came to him, he was up for grabs. The countless receipts and numbers I found in his suit pockets confirmed it. And then I'd gone and married him after being caught up in the lust of our biggest argument to date.

Last year, a woman, an actual voice to the suspicions I'd been having, called the apartment we shared, asking to speak with him. Her voice was thick with lust and desire. Then, she dared to call me his secretary. That was the last time I'd come home. I was too embarrassed and ashamed to let Vivian and Lisa know the real reason, so I told them I had to help get my little big brother out of trouble. My mama let me heal, cry on her shoulder, and kept me fed while I hid out in my childhood bedroom.

I lasted a few days until I finally answered one of Kenneth's nonstop calls. I drove back to Houston and walked into our apartment, my heart breaking when I saw the pitiful way Kenneth looked up at me when I walked into the living room. He told me he was sorry and begged me to forgive him. He then proposed to me right on the spot and said he'd marry me right then and there if I promised never to leave him again.

So, I forced his hand. A few days later, we repeated the standard-issue vows at the Harris County Courthouse. He'd gotten me this tennis bracelet, foregoing rings until we told our friends and families.

A secret that held stronger than his commitment to me.

The cashier handed Kenneth a receipt. He grabbed the bags with one hand, using his other to hold mine. I shot lasers at Vivian as we walked back to my car. She tried hiding behind her husband's height, but it was useless. Kenneth passed the bag to Lisa as I jerked my hand free.

"I hope the two of you get sick," I spat, walking over to the driver's side.

"Girl, why are you mad at me?" Lisa asked, flicking her gaze between Trent and me.

"Risse, I know what this looks like, but I promise it's not what you think," Vivian fretted.

"So, how else did the three musketeers know to come here?" Everyone looked around at each other before their gazes settled on Trent.

"Okay, so I may have let it slip. But it was an accident, I swear." Trent shrugged his shoulders, walking over to Lisa and wrapping an arm around her shoulders.

"Really, Lisa? I expected this from Viv, but you?" I seethed. "You know what, y'all can stay with them negroes. I'm out." I opened the car door and slammed it shut, settling into the seat. Kenneth tapped on the window, signaling me to let him in. I rolled down my window. "What the hell do you want, Kenneth?"

"Let me in the car, Risse," he said between his teeth.

"Hell no." I revved the engine, ready to drive off.

Kenneth gripped the door handle, leaning his head into the thin window crack. "Charisse, open the damn door."

"I said hell no. Now, unless you want me to drag your black ass up the street, I suggest you let go of the door." I revved the engine again, sealing my threat. *This negro got me out here acting crazy.*

"If that gets my wi–" he started.

"Get in!" I yelled, popping the locks to the door.

He climbed into the car, leaning the seat back as he extended his long frame in the passenger seat. I drove off, leaving our friends to figure out the rest of their day.

I drove around the streets of Treme, eventually ending up in New Orleans East. The car was silent. Kenneth burned a hole in my cheek the entire way, his long arm wrapped around the back of my seat.

"Talk to me, Risse." His voice was so rough yet sweet. His thumb brushed the back of my neck. I swallowed hard, trying to check the feelings welling up inside of me. I stopped at a red light, looking out of my window, and noticed a snowball stand to my left.

"Fine, but I'm getting a snowball first."

After parking in the shallow parking lot of the stand, Kenneth rushed out of the car to place our orders. He came back just as fast, handing me a small styrofoam cup piled high with soft ice covered in strawberry syrup and condensed milk. He had a slightly larger cup with orange syrup. It was our standard order whenever we visited a stand. We took a few bites, the soft static of the radio playing in the background.

"So what, Risse? You just gonna run home every time we argue now? That's how this marriage works?"

I sucked some of the syrup from my spoon, stalling. "Marriage works when two people respect each other."

Kenneth scoffed. "Oh, so now I don't respect you?"

"Do you?" I shot back, meeting his gaze. "Because last time I checked, flirting with other women in my face ain't exactly respectful."

He sighed, rubbing a hand over his head. A tingle went through my body as I watched the way his muscles rippled from the movement. "Charisse, I wasn't flirting. I was talking. You always assume the worst."

"Because you give me reasons to!" My voice came out sharper than I intended, and I felt a few heads turn our way from the stand.

Kenneth clenched his jaw, his grip on his cup tightening. "You think I want anybody but you? You think I'd be out here chasing you down if I didn't love you?"

I looked away, my heart pounding. "Love isn't enough, Kenneth. Not if I can't trust you."

Silence stretched between us, thick and suffocating. Kenneth exhaled, his voice softer this time. "Then let me fix it. Tell me how."

I didn't answer right away. Could he fix it? Could we fix it?

Finally, I sighed. "I don't know yet."

Kenneth stared at me for a long moment before nodding. "Alright. Then I'll wait. But I'm not leaving here until then. You're not leaving me, Charisse. We're married. That means something."

I swallowed hard, watching as he went back to eating his snowball. Who was he to tell me what I was or wasn't going to do?

"We'll see."

Kenneth smirked, looking back at me and then at his cup. "Yeah, we will."

I focused on the melting ice and syrup swirling in my cup, my heart tangled in knots. Because I knew one thing for certain.

This wasn't over.

Not even close.

Vivian

"I Love Me Some Him" - Toni Braxton

THE SCENT OF BARBECUE smoke mixed with the thick, humid air as we pulled up to Ms. Sonya's house. The sound of bounce music blared from speakers propped up on milk crates, blending with the voices of kids running up and down the block. The whole community was alive. Older men sat on concrete porches drinking cold beers, and grown women caught up in plastic lawn chairs, fanning themselves with folded newspapers. It was New Orleans in its rawest, most beautiful form.

Lisa was the first to climb out of the car, stretching her arms over her head. "Damn, Risse didn't say anything about a block party."

Trent smirked, adjusting the sleeves of his linen shirt. "Probably wanted to stay away, knowing this was the first place Kenneth was coming." He grazed his hand up Lisa's arm, giving her a wink. "You would've been too bougie to appreciate it, anyway."

Lisa shot him a look, but there was a tease in it. "Please, you aren't even from here."

Douglass let out a low chuckle, the sound rolling smooth and warm like honey. "Trent, you're always trying to act like you got deep New Orleans roots. You're from Baton Rouge."

Trent placed a hand over his chest. "That's supposed to be an insult?"

Lisa laughed, shaking her head, and I didn't miss the way Trent's eyes lingered on her just a second too long. There was something in the way he looked at her tonight, something playful but deliberate. Lisa pretended not to notice, but I knew better. Homegirl was feeling him, just as she did during college, even though she played hard to get.

Douglass touched the small of my back, a subtle but grounding touch. "You alright?"

"Yeah," I nodded. "Better that you're here, even if you can't keep your mouth closed for shit," I laughed, grazing a finger over Douglass' lips. He met my touch, swiping my lips, then following the touch with his. If I were a reckless woman, I'd let him have me right here in this courtyard, in front of everyone.

"I just want you to breathe, Vivi. I'm here. Ain't no rush to figure everything out. Not tonight, not this weekend. I just want you to enjoy yourself and your girls. We got time."

"I know, Doug," I exhaled.

He reached out, tucking a piece of hair behind my ear. "And you need to stop thinking so damn much."

I laughed softly, nudging him. "What are you, a therapist now?"

"Maybe I should start charging." His grin deepened before his gaze softened. "You know I got you, right?"

I exhaled slowly, letting the warmth of his voice settle against my skin. Douglass had that effect—steady, easy—a man who knew how to handle things without making a show of it. There was no insecurity in him, no bravado, just presence. I let myself lean into it.

"Come on," he said, brushing his fingers against mine before lacing them together. "Let's enjoy the night."

As the night stretched on, the block party grew livelier. The bounce music pulsed through the pavement, kids ran wild with sparklers, and Ms. Sonya's yard filled with people catching up over plates of food and trays of hot and spicy crawfish. Douglass and I danced nonstop, his arms locked around my waist as we grooved to hits by Partners N Crime, DJ Jimi, and Juvenile. For once, I felt at ease, just letting the rhythm of the night carry my stresses away with the Mississippi River. I was going to need to get my hair done as soon as we got back to Houston, with the way my hair was sweated out from the heat in the air and my body.

I let Douglass pull me through the crowds, stopping every few feet to speak with some of the older folk sitting outside. He had that effortless charm that made people gravitate toward him, laughing and joking as if he'd known them his whole life. Watching him, I was reminded of the reasons I fell in love with him in the first place. He never rushed me, never pressured me to say more than I was ready to.

He just...knew.

After making a few rounds and throwing back a few beers and wine coolers, we ended up on a porch a few doors down from Ms. Sonya's house, just far enough from the loudest speaker. He leaned against the railing, sipping from his beer before looking at me with low eyes and that knowing smile. After taking another sip, he bit his lip, his eyes crinkling. I knew what that look meant, and so did the burning furnace between my legs.

I looked up at my husband. *My husband*. How the hell did I end up with this 6'4", quiet storm of a man? Even though he wore a short-sleeve t-shirt with navy chino shorts, I could see the power in his arms and thighs.

"You staying at Ms. Sonya's tonight?" he asked, his gaze low and warm. His tongue ran over his bottom lip again.

"Probably," I replied, glancing toward the rest of the courtyard. "This is supposed to be a girls' weekend, remember?" I stared back into his eyes, challenging him.

"I don't like that." He kneeled, his fingers brushing the side of my face. "Come stay with me instead."

I raised an eyebrow. "And share a room with you and those fools. Absolutely not," I laughed, shaking my head.

"I got my own room. Figured I'd be more comfortable that way," he said with a slow grin. "Because if you thought I was going to sleep alone, with my wife in the same city, you thought wrong."

I bit my lip, considering. I know Charisse needed Lisa and me, but other than that, there wasn't a single reason to say no. And, when Douglass looked at me like that – sex dripping from his eyes – it was damn near impossible.

"Alright," I said, my voice softer than I meant it.

His grin deepened. "Good."

Douglass swooped me in his arms, taking my place on the porch and resting me over his thighs. I chugged the remainder of his beer as he nuzzled his face in the crook of my neck, nipping my ear lobes and neck. The thick hair tickled my sensitive spot something good.

As he continued the assault on my neck, I looked out into the courtyard again. I could see everything, including the moment Charisse and Kenneth arrived. Charisse was stiff as she charged toward her mother's house. Kenneth kept up with her pace, his lips moving low and fast, trying to work his way back into her good graces. It was a dance I'd seen them do too many times.

Douglass sighed beside me. "Here we go. I told his ass to let her breathe."

I crossed my arms, watching as Charisse's face twisted, her patience thinning. "I don't know why he thinks he can just talk his way back in."

Douglass chuckled, but there was a knowing edge to it. "Because he always has."

He wasn't wrong. Charisse and Kenneth had a gravity to them. He always pulled her back in, no matter how hard she tried to push him away. Ms. Sonya's voice cut through the tension.

"Kenneth, boy, you better not be over there harassing my baby in front of everybody."

A few people laughed, and Kenneth sucked his teeth, but backed off, shaking his head. Charisse didn't move, but I could see the tension in her shoulders. Kenneth made his way toward us, his chest puffed up under his white tank, tucked snugly into his jean shorts.

"Let's roll out," he huffed, slapping Douglass on the shoulder.

"Let me go see what's going on with this fool," Douglas said, kissing me on my shoulder. He stood, placing me on the ground. I pouted my lips as he walked away with Kenneth, Trent joining them as they made their way to Douglass's car.

Just as they pulled off, another car pulled up to the curb. A shiny black Lexus with custom rims, the engine humming like it owned the block. A man stepped out, draped in gold chains, a white undershirt hugging his broad chest. Basketball shorts hung low on his hips as he brought a 40 oz. bottle of malt liquor to his lips. Confidence rolled off him in waves, the kind of energy that turned heads without him even trying.

PJ.

Ms. Sonya crossed her arms from the porch. "Ain't I lucky? I got both my children under my roof at the same time. Charisse," Ms. Sonya yelled. "Come say hi to your brother?"

The second I saw PJ, I knew we were in for a long night. I stood beside Lisa and Charisse, meeting up by Ms. Sonya's porch. PJ strolled up like he owned the whole damn block, nodding at a few of his boys before locking eyes with all of us. Charisse shifted back and forth on her feet, annoyed with her brother's presence, even though it'd only been minutes since he'd arrived.

"Wazzam," he started, his voice drawling. "If it ain't my lil' sis."

Charisse rolled her eyes. "PJ, I'm older than you."

"You keep rolling them eyes, they gon' get stuck like that." He gave her a once over, his expression tightening. "Where Doc at? You still runnin' behind that nigga?"

"PJ, not tonight."

"Nah, see, it gotta be tonight." He stepped closer to her face, lowering his voice. "Every time I turn around, you making dumb ass choices that don't make no goddamn sense."

Charisse clenched her jaw. "I don't need you telling me how to live my life."

PJ let out a humorless chuckle. "You do."

"Look, PJ," Charisse started, placing her hands on her hips, poking an acrylic nail in the center of PJ's chest. "Last time I checked, you still slanging dope on the block. Is that the life you want me to live? Why can't you admit I'm doing better?"

Lisa and I moved closer to Ms. Sonya's door while her kids duked it out. Charisse and PJ stared at each other for a long beat before he exhaled and shook his head. He wrapped Charisse in his arms, his looming body engulfing her frame. After a second, Charisse hugged her brother back, a smile blossoming on both their faces.

"You know I respect you for going off to college and getting up outta here. But, I ain't gon' watch you waste yourself on a nigga that don't deserve you." PJ gave Charisse another hug, then fist-bumped her shoulder. "If I find out Doc fucking up, he gon' have to see me."

Charisse smacked her lips, pulling back. "Ain't nobody fucking up, PJ."

PJ grunted. "Yeah, aight." He turned to meet with a few of his boys, who walked over. "I meant what I said, Risse," he yelled over his shoulder.

As he disappeared into the crowd, Charisse turned to Lisa and me. "Let's go out. I need to clear my head."

"Risse, this whole trip is supposed to be you clearing your head," Lisa whined.

"And yet, it was your big mouth that told Trent we were here." Charisse brushed past us as she entered the house, and Lisa and I followed closely behind. Whatever plans she had for us tonight, I hoped they'd be over soon. My husband was waiting for me, and no matter how big the guilt trip Charisse would send me on, I wasn't missing out on that.

Lisa

"I'm Your Baby Tonight" - Whitney Houston

THE CLUB PULSED WITH life, the bass line of a classic New Orleans bounce track vibrating through the air, wrapping around my skin like the humid night outside. Neon lights flickered against glossy, deep-red walls, and the floor was packed with bodies moving to the rhythm, hips rolling, shoulders bouncing. It smelled like expensive perfume, Hennesy, and sweat, the kind of night where anything could happen.

I smoothed a hand down the silk slip dress hugging my body, deep emerald green, with a high slit that skimmed the top of my thigh. Charisse's bamboo earrings brushed my jaw as I tossed my hair back, scanning the club with amusement. Vivian, in a form-fitting black dress, sipped her cocktail beside me, while Charisse, in a short, hot-pink mini dress with mesh cutouts, rolled her eyes at the man beside her.

"Wazzam, baby. I just wanna dance witcha' one time," he pleaded, already halfway tipsy, his gold teeth glinting under the strobe lights.

Charisse cocked her hip. "And I already told you, no."

He put his hands up in surrender. "Aight, aight. I see how it is." He backed off, but not before giving her one last once over, muttering something about her being stuck up before slinking into the crowd.

Vivian chuckled. "If you wanted to break hearts all weekend, you could've just said that."

Charisse scoffed. "If they have a weak heart, that's their problem."

I took a sip of my Hurricane, licking the sweetness off my lips before tilting my head. "At least he tried. The last guy that came up to you, you didn't even let him finish his sentence."

Charisse lifted her glass. "Because I already knew he wasn't the one."

Vivian sighed, already knowing the answer to her next question. "And who is the one?"

Charisse raised an eyebrow. "Y'all are being really sentimental right now. Drink some more liquor."

"Girl, it's your emotional ass that has us out here anyway," I laughed, sipping my drink.

Charisse smirked, nudging Vivian's shoulder. "We all got our shit we've been carrying around, acting like it doesn't weigh a ton. It's not just me running from Kenneth. Viv's dealing with...well, everything, and you? You're about to walk into a wedding that feels more wrong than it does right."

Vivian set her drink down, tilting her head. "Lisa, when she's right, she's right. Do you want to marry Wesley Wright?" The way Vivian said his name mirrored the uncertainty I had surrounding the arrangement.

I let out a slow breath, running a finger along the rim of my glass. "It's not about wanting, Viv. It's about what makes sense. My family wants this. His family wants this. Everything is lined up perfectly."

"That's not a reason to marry somebody," Charisse scoffed.

"And how would you know?" I retorted, shooting Charisse a look. "You run here every time Kenneth does something. What would you know about making a marriage work?"

Charisse sucked her teeth but didn't argue. Instead, she tapped her nails against her glass, her voice softer. Vivian reached for her hand, squeezing it. "You know we got you, right? No matter what."

Charisse swallowed hard, nodding. "Yeah, I know."

I exhaled, feeling the gravity of our shared history settle between us. We didn't have separate struggles; we were never battling anything alone. No matter our paths or choices, we always returned to each other.

"Are you going to give him another chance?" I asked.

Before Charisse could answer, the air in the club shifted. I felt him before I saw them. The gravitational pull of men who knew exactly who they were, men who didn't need to ask for attention because it was handed to them the second they walked into the room.

Douglass, Kenneth. Trent.

Trenton Nathaniel Breaux.

Kenneth led the way, his chain swinging as he scanned the club, his sharp eyes locking onto Charisse like he had her GPS coordinates embedded into his soul. Douglass walked with his usual unbothered ease, his navy-blue silk shirt unbuttoned just enough to hint at the body underneath, his watch gleaming with subtle wealth. If Vivian hadn't clung to my arm for dear life, I'd swear she'd melted into a puddle on the floor.

And then there was Trent. His black t-shirt was crisp and tucked into the black slacks that hugged his thighs just right. A gold chain circled the collar of his shirt, glowing under the lights. As I traced my eyes back to his face, a smirk played on his lips, the green of his eyes locking with mine.

Oh, he was trouble.

And I wanted all of it.

He'd been toying with me all day, those lingering glances, the way his hand had brushed against my arm earlier at the block party. And now this, in this setting, with the heat turned up, the game had shifted.

Calm down, Lisa. You're getting married in a few months.

He didn't say a word as they made their way to our spot at the bar, as he walked up beside me, close enough that I could feel the warmth of his body, smell the lingering hint of his cologne, something deep and smooth, like sandalwood and spice.

"You been dodging me," he murmured.

I arched a brow, taking another slow sip of my drink. "I didn't realize we had an appointment."

Trent chuckled, a low, rich sound that sent a shiver down my spine. "You always got jokes."

I smirked, tilting my head. "And you always got a line."

"Ain't a line if it's the truth." His hand ghosted up the exposed skin of my thigh, barely touching, just teasing. "We always had something, Lisa. You just never let yourself see it."

I lifted a brow. "You call this something? You flirted with every woman with a pulse back in college."

He grinned. "Oh, I flirted. But none of them got under my skin like you. You know that."

I took another sip of my drink, keeping my face neutral even as my pulse jumped. "Sounds like revisionist history."

"Or maybe it's just the truth you didn't want to deal with." He leaned closer, his breath warm against my ear. "Where's your ring?"

"My what?"

"Ring," he confirmed, tapping my ring finger. "Isn't the bride supposed to have a ring? I know that Wright money runs deep. Where's the rock you got?"

I felt the naked space where I normally wore my engagement ring, realizing its weight had been absent since we left Houston. "I must've left it at home," I laughed nervously.

My stomach flipped. I should have pulled away. I should have shut this down. But the way he looked at me, like he had already decided how this night would end, had my pulse skipping beats. I held his gaze, letting the tension stretch between us like a drawn bowstring, waiting for release.

"Dance with me," he said, his voice smoother than the liquor in my glass.

"I don't think my fiancé would appreciate that," I replied, taking another sip, trying to quench the dryness of my mouth.

"You think I give a fuck about that," he commanded, biting his lip as he took my hand in his.

I hesitated long enough to make him wait before finishing the rest of my drink and setting the glass down. "One dance."

His grin was pure satisfaction as he took my hand, leading me onto the floor. The DJ switched the track, the beat of Jodeci's *Come & Talk to Me* rolling through the speakers, and Trent moved behind me, his hands settling on my waist.

I let him pull me into his rhythm, my back against his chest, our movements slow and deliberate. His grip tightened slightly, his breath warm against my ear.

"You keep playing with me, Lisa."

I pressed back against him, just enough to feel the solid weight of his body. "Who said I was playing?"

His fingers traced small circles along my hipbone, and I felt the heat coil low in my belly.

"Let's get out of here," he murmured.

I turned my head just enough to meet his gaze, dark and heavy with intent. His honey-toned skin glistened with a slight sheen of sweat from the packed club. His thick, pink lips, surrounded by dark hair groomed into a neat mustache and goatee, harkened to me like a drug. I should have said no. I should have thought about the fact that this was Trent. Trent, who always flirted, always pushed, always played the game but never quite crossed the line.

But tonight, I wanted the line obliterated.

I took his hand, letting him lead me through the crowd, slipping past Charisse and Kenneth. The two were locked in their own silent battle of wills. Vivian caught my eye and smirked knowingly. Trent and I barely made it to the sidewalk, before he pressed me up against a light pole, his hands firm on my ass, his lips hovering over mine.

"You sure about this?" he asked, his voice low, gravelly.

I curled my fingers into the fabric of his shirt, pulling him closer. "Stop talking."

His mouth crashed into mine, hot and demanding, and any last bit of hesitation burned away. He tasted like whiskey and heat, his hands gripping my thighs as he pressed the growing monster in his pants against my center.

I barely registered his flagging down a cab or the short drive to his hotel, my body buzzing with anticipation. The second the door shut behind us, Trent's hands tangled in my hair as he pinned me against it, his mouth claiming mine with a hunger that stole the breath from my lungs.

This was different.

This wasn't the slow, careful seduction I remembered from college. This was years of want, years of frustration, years of knowing that this should have been us.

"You think I forgot how you taste?" he growled against my lips, his fingers slipping under the hem of my dress, his touch a hot brand against my skin. He dropped to his knees, his hands trailing up my thighs, bunching my dress around my waist.

"You smell intoxicating," he murmured, pressing open-mouthed kisses along my inner thighs and over my soaked lace thong. "I don't think I'll ever get the smell and taste of you out of my system."

I smoothed my fingers over Dramamine waves he kept in check from the Murray's pomade I knew he'd used since the first night we studied together in his dorm. We'd gone from studying our textbooks to the inside of each other's mouths in a matter of hours. It could have gone further. I wanted it to go further. But I was scared then.

And now, with his head and tongue getting reacquainted with the flesh between the juncture of my thighs, that fear was at the bottom of a muddy swamp.

His thumb pulled down the lace of my panties, and his tongue swept between my lower lips, dripping in anticipation. "Been wanting to do this for a long time," he spoke into me, his breath caressing my slickened center, causing me to thrust my hips into his mouth again. My back bowed from the door, my fingers tightening on his head.

I gasped, rocking my hips into his mouth. "Then stop talking and do it."

And he did. He groaned as he devoured me, tongue stroking, teasing, tasting, like he had all the time in the world to make me come undone on his shoulders. I didn't realize I was moaning his name until I felt his fingers dig into my thighs, holding me steady.

His mouth was sinful, relentless, working me over with precision, with purpose, like he had memorized me years ago and was just now cashing in on all the ways he'd imagined breaking me apart.

I was already falling, unraveling, losing myself, when suddenly he pulled back, wiping his mouth with the back of his hand, his dark green eyes gleaming with satisfaction and something more dangerous – possession.

Before I could protest, he had me in his arms, lifting me effortlessly, my legs wrapping around his waist like second nature, his hands securely under my ass. His mouth found my neck, hot and wet, sucking just enough to make me whimper.

"Not too hard," I panted. "I don't want you to leave a mark."

He threw me on the bed, grinning down at me. "Can't have the future Mrs. Wright getting caught up, can we?" He chuckled, but the edge in his voice made my stomach clench.

I leaned back on my elbows, stuck in the domineering way he peered down at me, letting my dress ride up my thighs, watching him watch me. He could ask me to do whatever, and I would. Slowly, he peeled his shirt from his torso in one smooth motion, the muscles along his stomach rippling along the way. He did that chest jump thing that made me squeeze down low, becoming all too familiar with the ache he'd left when he'd removed his lips from mine.

Lord, have mercy.

His body was all muscle, all heat, all temptation, and I was drowning in it.

He unbuckled his belt, slowly lowering the zipper on his pants, kicking off his shoes as the pants dropped to the floor. He was thick, hard, already straining against the fabric of his boxers. His teeth grazed his bottom lip as he crouched toward me, slow, methodical. A lion eyeing up its prey before the kill.

His body knelt over mine, his fingers grazing my neck and shoulder, then pulled the thin strap of my dress down, exposing my breasts. Little chill bumps raised around the exposed flesh, only subsiding once his firm hands swept across my skin. When he squeezed them, I moaned, raising my hips toward him.

"Lisa, look at me." I opened my eyes, looking at this beautiful man: the squareness of his jaw, the strength of his shoulders, the heat of his eyes. Taunting me. Teasing me.

"Trent, you're doing a lot of talking tonight. If you can't back it up, just say that."

The laugh that left his lips must have escaped from the pits of hell. He snatched the dress from my body, pulling it over my head, leaving me bare beneath him. He assaulted my body with burning lashes of his tongue, going from my neck down to my core, yearning for him. The traces of his hands were scorching, sweeping over my curves, teasing, taking, claiming. Our bodies grew slick with a sheen of sweat, even as the hotel's AC continued on full blast.

Trent grabbed my chin, tilting my head to meet his, sucking my lips into his. His kiss was rough, hungry, sensual. He was devouring me, claiming me, showing me exactly who I belonged to in this moment. And I was a willing participant.

I moaned into his mouth, arching into him, my body desperate for more. His hands gripped my hips, fingers digging into my skin as he rocked against me, teasing me with what was coming next.

"Let me make one thing clear," he murmured against my lips. "I talk a lot of shit, but you know damn well I ain't ever been the type to make promises I can't keep." He ground his hips against my soaked core. "And tonight, I'm gonna make sure you don't forget that." With his last words, he freed his dick from his boxers, my eyes widening at the thick mushroom of the head.

"Nah, Mrs. Wright, don't get scared now." The Cheshire Cat would be jealous of the grin pasted on his face right now.

"Tell me when you're ready," he growled. Kneeling between my thighs, he let his fingers explore the depths of my desire, the digits massaging my walls, my readiness making itself known around the room. Each time my walls clenched down on his fingers, he grunted and stroked his penis.

"I'm ready," I panted, my hips moving in tandem with the pace he set with his hand.

"Nah," he laughed. "It don't seem like you're ready yet." Trent increased his pace, that damn smile growing brighter, more arrogant.

My breath grew ragged. My hands dug into the sheets as I felt my climax coming. I wanted to hold on, tried to hold on. I didn't want to come this way. I wanted him inside of me, working me out, imprinting his dick so deep inside I'd have a lifetime of memories to get me through this facade of a marriage.

"Tell me when you're ready, Lisa," he said, his voice growing raspy.

"Fuck, Trent," I cried, tears pricking the corners of my eyes. "Please. I can't hold on any longer."

He continued to stroke me with his fingers as he grabbed a condom from his wallet on the nightstand, sheathing himself.

Anticipation hung in the air.

I watched as he positioned himself between my thighs, dragging his length along my slickened lips, teasing me, his favorite game.

And then, he pushed into me, slow, deep, deliberate.

The stretch was too much and not enough, my body tightening, clenching, needing.

He groaned. I gasped.

And then he started to move.

The slow wave of pain and pleasure coursed through my body, snatching my soul and bringing me back to life. I was mesmerized by the ripple of his abs as he stroked into me. First slow, deep strokes followed quick, shallow thrusts that took my breath. His hands gripped my hips tight, controlling them, controlling me. It was a sin and a shame that my body was reacting to his touch.

"Umph, if I had known it'd be like this, I wouldn't have waited until you were about to say "*I do.*'" Trent leaned back on his knees, pulling me up to straddle his thighs. He bounced me along his dick as I wrapped my hands around his neck, holding on for the ride. His lips buried themselves against my neck, bringing forth another mind-shattering tingling throughout my body. I held his head in place as I wound my hips to meet his. I was close, so close. Just a few more–

"Fuck," I cried, my back arching as euphoria coursed through my body. Trent's movements became uncontrolled as I squeezed tight around him, letting the high of my orgasm run its course. A few seconds later, he growled into my neck, squeezing my body closer to his as he found his release.

We stayed locked in each other's arms, trying to catch our breath. Once we'd come down, Trent got off the bed and pulled me into his arms, carrying me into the bathroom. He started the shower, where I relaxed against his body as he washed us both. He carried me to the bed, where I snuggled into his arms.

This moment was everything I knew it would be.

And that was a damn shame.

Because it couldn't happen again.

Charisse

"Love Shoulda Brought You Home" - Toni Braxton

ID HE HAVE A tracker on me that I didn't know about?

Bass-heavy beats moved the crowd on the dance floor from side to side, threatening to swallow a person whole and spit them back out. And Kenneth was right in the center of it, stalking toward me like he had something to prove.

I took another slow sip of my drink, my fingers tightening around the glass. I didn't want to see him, didn't want to feel the way my pulse jumped the second our eyes locked, but there he was, his chain swinging, his energy too big for the packed club. He was sexy. Too damn sexy in that gray pinstripe suit and white shirt. And I saw them, the vultures he passed on the dance floor.

But only I had his eyes, as he made his way to me, one hand shoved in his pocket like he had all the damn time in the world.

"Why do you keep me looking for you?" he said, his voice smooth, but his eyes gave him away. There was something behind the smooth exterior, something restless, something breaking.

I set my drink down, exhaling sharply. "And I've been trying not to be found."

"Yeah?" Kenneth bit his lip, smoothing a hand over his mustache. "That's why you out here looking like that?" His eyes dragged over my body, slow and intentional, like he still had a right to do that. "You were waiting on me, weren't you?"

"Ha," I laughed, sharp and quick. "Negro, please."

But he was undeterred, stepping closer, close enough that I could still smell the familiar mix of his cologne with the Hennesy lingering on his tongue. Close enough that my body remembered before my mind could catch up.

"Why you fighting me so hard, Risse baby?" His voice was low now, just for me. "You know you still mine."

I stiffened. "I stopped being yours a little over a week ago."

Kenneth licked his lips, his jaw ticking. "Then say it."

My stomach flipped, but I kept my face blank. "Say what?"

"That you don't love me."

The words sliced through me, clean and deep, because I wanted to say them. I wanted to look him dead in his face and tell him that whatever we had was dead, that I was over it, over him. That I had moved on.

But we both knew I couldn't.

Not yet.

He saw it, the hesitation, the moment of weakness, and stepped even closer. "That's what I thought."

The DJ switched tracks, the infamous *Triggerman* beat rolling through the speakers, setting the club on fire. People were moving harder now, intensified. Sweat-slicked bodies pressed together on the dance floor.

I needed to get away from him. *Now.*

I turned to walk away, but Kenneth caught my wrist, his grip gentle but firm. "Charisse."

I didn't look at him. *Couldn't.* "Let me go, Kenneth."

His fingers flexed, holding me for half a second longer before he exhaled through his nose, loosening his grip. "Not yet."

I closed my eyes, inhaling through my nose, steadying myself. "You don't get to do this anymore."

"I don't?" His voice dipped lower, something vulnerable creeping in. "Then why are you still here? Why are we still here?"

I opened my mouth, but no words came. Because I was here, wasn't I? And that was the problem. I was always here. A sitting duck for him to return to after his latest fling. No protesting, digesting each indiscretion like the medicine he prescribed to his patients. And with every fill, a piece of myself chipped away. How many more times until there was nothing left of me?

Kenneth leaned in, his lips barely brushing my ear. His hands circled my waist, kneading into the soft flesh of my hips, taunting me, teasing me. "Can we talk, Risse baby? Please." And that was my undoing, the subtle crack of his voice as he made his plea.

And despite every rational thought telling me to walk away, I followed him.

The air outside was cooler but not by much. The thick humidity pressed against my skin, mixing with the sweat already clinging to my body from being inside. Streetlights flickered overhead, and the muffled bass of the club still pulsed through the night.

Kenneth leaned against the side wall of the shotgun house, his hands sliding into his pockets, his head tilting as he watched me. "You still mad at me?"

"I'm not mad." I crossed my arms, my nostrils flaring. "I'm hurt, Kenneth."

He nodded, lips pressing together like he knew it, too. "I know I'm not perfect, baby."

"Perfect? Kenneth, you ain't even close! You got the nerve to stand here, lookin' at me like I'm supposed to be impressed that you came chasin' after me, like that fixes all the times you disrespected me right in my damn face! Like that undoes the times you made me feel like I was crazy for callin' you out on your shit!"

He flinched but didn't interrupt.

I stepped closer, my anger boiling over, my voice rising above the night air. "You think love is enough? That I'm just supposed to forget how many times you embarrassed me? How many times have you made me feel like I wasn't enough? All the women I've had to answer to because of you. I'm tired, Kenneth! I'm tired of feeling like I gotta fight for a man who don't fight for me the same way!" Tears brimmed in my eyes as my vision went blurry.

Kenneth ran a hand over his face, frustration flickering in his eyes. "Charisse, I never-"

"You never what?" I cut him off, my voice cracking. "Never meant to hurt me? Never meant to let your ego be more important than us? Never meant to have me out here questioning my worth? You got me out here comparing myself to these heifers that call the house when you're at the hospital. The ones shaking their ass in your face when you stare a second too long. What's going to come next, Kenneth? A child that's not mine. Is all that worth us?"

"Baby, it wasn't my intention to-" he started, taking steps toward me.

"Fuck you and your intentions! I don't give a damn about your intentions, Kenneth! Intentions don't change the way I cry myself to sleep some nights, wondering when you'll get home. Wondering if I was just another thing for you to conquer instead of cherish. You were supposed to cherish me. Me. Your wife!"

Silence fell between us, thick and suffocating.

Kenneth's chest rose and fell hard, his jaw tight, his fists clenched at his sides. But his eyes, those damn eyes, weren't just frustrated anymore.

They were breaking.

I saw the moment hit him, the heaviness of it all. The realization that this time, he might not be able to smooth-talk his way back. This time, my anger wasn't just a storm waiting to pass. This time, he had truly pushed me too far. Past my breaking point. Past my point of no return.

He swallowed hard, stepping back like my words had sucker-punched him in the gut. "I'm sorry, baby."

"Is that supposed to be an apology?" I let out a sharp laugh. "Fuck your apology, Kenneth!"

"Dammit, Risse!" He ran a hand over his face, exasperated. "Tell me what you need!"

I shook my head. "You don't get to do this, Kenneth. You don't get to pop up with some half-ass sorry and act like I'm supposed to fall back in line!"

"I never wanted you in line!" he yelled back, his voice rougher now. "I wanted you with me. I wanted to know you were in this just as much as I am!" He paced back and forth, trying to steady his temper. "How do you think I feel after every little thing I do that you don't agree with, you run back home to your mother and brother? You're supposed to be my wife, and you throw me away any chance you get!"

I swallowed, my throat tightening. "Then why do you keep hurting me?"

He went quiet, his feet stilling. And for the first time in a long time, Kenneth didn't have an answer.

I turned to walk away, my heels clicking against the pavement. *Don't look back. Don't look back.*

"Baby."

I kept walking, seeing my car just up the way. Kenneth's footsteps echoed behind me. No matter how loud the music on Frenchman Street was, I would always hear him, always feel his presence like a mosquito hovering before making its mark.

"Charisse."

I stopped just in front of my car door. My hand hovered over the handle. His voice was different as he called my name. Hollow. Desperate.

"Charisse, I don't want anybody else," he said, his voice cracking slightly. I could feel him staring at me from the curb on the other side of my car. "I just want you."

I inhaled deeply, my heart slamming against my ribs. *You know he means it. You always know when he's telling the truth.*

"You have to mean that in the way it matters, Kenneth. Not just when you're scared to lose me." I turned my face up slightly, just enough to see him from the corner of my eye. He didn't say anything, but the look in his eyes was enough to knock the wind out of me.

I opened my car door, sank into the seat, and started the engine, ready to make my final escape. I had to, needed to, get away before he said anything else.

Because if he had?

I might've stayed.

Kenneth

"I'm Still In Love With You" - New Edition

THE RAIN HIT THE pavement in thick, heavy drops, soaking through my clothes by the time I climbed out of the cab. I didn't care. I had bigger things to worry about than being wet. My heart was hammering in my chest as I stared at the porch light glowing behind the curtains of Charisse's mother's house.

This was it.

I spent the whole ride here thinking about what to say and how to fix this. Every word felt too small, too meaningless. But I had to try. Because if I lost Charisse now, it would be for good.

I knocked hard and fast. My stomach twisted as I waited, the seconds stretching too long. I was about to knock again when the door swung open.

Ms. Sonya stood there, her eyes almost level with mine. It blew me away how much she looked like her daughter, or rather, how much Charisse favored her. Same almond-shaped eyes, the same toffee-colored skin. Her mother stood there, barefoot in the warm glow of the living room, her arms folded tight over her chest. Her eyes scanned me, filled with disapproval, as I stood on her porch, looking like the damn fool that I was.

"You look stupid as hell standing out here in the rain," she said, her voice flat.

"Yeah, probably," I laughed dryly.

Even with the rain continuing to pelt my back, she made no effort to move. Didn't invite me in. Just stood there like a brick wall. But she hadn't shut the door in my face, so I still had a chance.

"Ms. Sonya, can I come in? I need to talk to Risse. Please." That last word came out hoarse. I rubbed my face, feeling a wetness there, some rain, some tears.

"You better hope my son don't come back no time soon." Ms. Sonya backed away from the door, leaving me barely six inches to cross the threshold. "Risse, bring your ass out here. Bringing all this damn drama to my doorstep."

I held my breath as I heard the soft tap of footsteps coming from the back. When she tiptoed into the living room, a soft exhale left my chest. I took her in, the smooth peanut butter of her skin, her curves on display in the pink mini-dress she wore. She lifted her head, her eyes meeting mine. Her hair was still in the curly updo from earlier, the bang still sweeping across her forehead. Her eyes were puffy and swollen, raw with emotion.

"Y'all got about thirty minutes 'til PJ come back." Ms. Sonya looked between the two of us before huffing and walking to the back of her home.

Charisse looked back at me, a few lingering tears still sitting on her lower lashes.

"I can't lose you," I said, my voice rough. "I can't. I won't."

She exhaled, shaking her head, the tears escaping down her round cheeks. "Kenneth, you already did."

"No." I stepped forward, dripping water onto the linoleum floor. "Not yet. Not if you're still standing here, listening."

She sighed, rubbing her temples. "I should make you leave."

"But you won't," I pushed. "Because you know this isn't over."

Her lips pressed into a thin line. I could see the battle happening inside her, the war between her heart and her pride. Before she could say anything else, I did the one thing I had never done before. Not even when I asked her to be my wife, my forever.

I dropped to my knees.

Her eyes widened. "Kenneth-"

"I know I messed up," I said, gripping her hands before she could pull away. "I know I haven't been the man I should've been for you. But, Risse baby, I swear to God, I ain't ever stop loving you. Not for a second."

She yanked her hands back, her voice cracking. "Love ain't enough, Kenneth. It's never been enough."

"I know," I said quickly, desperately. "I know that. And I'm not asking you to take me back just because I love you. I'm asking you to give me one more chance to prove that I can be better. That I can be the man you deserve."

She turned away, pressing the heels of her hands into her eyes. "Kenneth, I'm tired."

I stood behind her, pulling her close to my chest. "I know, baby," I murmured into her ear. "I know. And I hate that I'm the reason for that." I took a deep breath. "But if you give me one more chance, just one more, I swear I will never make you feel like this again."

She swallowed hard, her back still to me. "Why now? What'll be different this time around?"

I pressed my soaked face against the crook of her neck, grabbing her wrist, wrapping her tight in my arms. "Because I finally understand what it feels like to lose you. And I don't want to live with that. I can't live with that."

She turned in my arms as the front door creaked open behind me. PJ.

I turned and tucked her behind me. As her brother stepped inside, his eyes locked on me like a loaded gun. The air in the room shifted, heavy and dangerous. I knew this was coming.

"The fuck going on in here?" His lips curled as he grabbed the strap tucked at his waist.

I squared my shoulders. "PJ, leave Risse and me alone so we can talk."

PJ flicked his eyes at his sister. "Nah, yo' bitch ass need to get the fuck out my mama house. Ya' heard me?"

I clenched my jaw. "I ain't leaving unless Risse comes with me."

"The hell you not." PJ stepped closer, tension radiating off him. "You don't get to run through my sister life, fuckin' up her peace. I'll put you six feet deep before I let you do that, Doc."

Ms. Sonya returned to the front room, hearing PJ and me. Charisse tugged at my arm. I faintly heard her tell me to leave before things got worse.

"This ain't about you," I said, my voice tight.

PJ let out a bitter laugh. "Nah, see, that's where you got it twisted. Everything that affects her, I handle."

"PJ, calm your ass down, yelling in my house like this," Ms. Sonya yelled from her spot next to Charisse.

I stepped to PJ, leveling my face with his. "I'm the only one handling things behind my wife."

Gasps sounded behind me, but I kept my eyes on PJ.

"Fuck you say, nigga!" PJ's face twisted up as my words settled around the room. "Fuck he talkin' 'bout Risse?"

I turned to face my wife, seeing her tremble next to her mother. Her eyes darted between PJ and me. I saw the silent plea for me to take back the words I'd just spoken. But I wouldn't. If we were to move forward, everything needed to be out in the open, fuck what everyone thought.

"Risse, is this man your husband?" Her mother glared at her, hands on her hips, her eyes piercing, searching for the truth.

"M-m-mama—" she stuttered, eyes wide.

Ms. Sonya turned to face me. "Boy, you better be joking."

"Ain't no joke, Ms. Sonya," I said, squaring my shoulders. "Charisse is my wife."

"Risse, yo' ass better get to talking," PJ shifted, his body already humming with anger. "When the fuck this happen? And, why you ain't said shit?"

"It happened months ago," I admitted.

Ms. Sonya let out a sharp, disapproving scoff. "You mean to tell me, you done went off and married this man, and couldn't give your own mama the courtesy of knowing?"

"Because..." Charisse's voice was tight, barely above a whisper. "I knew how y'all would react."

"Nah, keep all that quiet shit, Risse. It's too late to be acting all ashamed, now."

"It's not like that–"

"Oh, it's exactly like that!" Ms. Sonya cut her off, shaking her head in disbelief. "You hid this from us for a reason, Charisse, and don't you dare act like you didn't."

"Because y'all never gave him a chance." Charisse's voice cracked as she spoke. "I love him. Why does this even matter?"

"Love?" Ms. Sonya's face twisted in disgust. "Love don't mean keeping secrets from your family. Love ain't you running home after every argument. You gon' let a man put a ring on your finger and not even look your family in the eye?"

"Nah, Mama. Unless my eyes playing tricks on me, I don't see no ring," PJ added.

"Hush, PJ." Charisse wiped her face, her voice shaking. "I didn't say anything, because I didn't want to lose y'all."

"But you was real fine choosing him over us." PJ scoffed, shaking his head.

My patience snapped. The only reason we were in this mess was because Charisse wanted to wait for the perfect moment to tell them, so they wouldn't react like this. "She didn't choose anything. She's mine, and I'm hers. And, I hope y'all would respect that."

I felt PJ pacing behind me. "See, that's where you got me fucked up. That's my sister, and everything to do with her got something to do with me!"

"Then I guess that's a problem you gonna have to figure out!"

I turned to face PJ, barely seeing the punch coming.

His fist cracked against my jaw, snapping my head to the side. The metallic taste of blood filled my mouth, but I stayed on my feet, wiping it away with the back of my hand.

And then, I swung back.

The room exploded into chaos. I barely heard Charisse and Ms. Sonya yelling as we grabbed at each other, fists flying. We crashed into the coffee table, knocking over a lamp. PJ swung again, and I dodged, shoving him back.

"Mama, stop him!" Charisse yelled in the background.

The screen door burst open, and we tumbled into the yard, rain pelting us from above. PJ lunged, tackling me to the ground, fist raining down. I rolled us over, landing my hits, the rain mixing with sweat and blood.

"I should been beat yo' ass for the way you been treatin' my sister, nigga."

I laughed, bitter and breathless. "Too bad. I ain't going anywhere."

"Fuck you say, nigga?" I moved to swing again, but PJ caught my wrist, pulling me into a headlock. Seconds later, I felt the cold metal of his gun tight against my temple. "Say something else. I'll lay yo' ass out right here."

"PJ!" Ms. Sonya and Charisse shrieked from their place on the porch.

"PJ, stop! Both of you stop!" Charisse cried, running toward us.

"Give me the word, Risse!"

We froze.

I looked up, rain pouring down my face. Charisse stood a few feet away, her arms wrapped around herself, her face twisted in something close to heartbreak.

I huffed and puffed, staring into Charisse's soul. The thundering sound of rain hitting the ground and buildings around us faded as my life was in her hands. It always was. Whether she believed it or not, she had the power to break me. I guess that's why a part of me fought so hard to give myself fully to her.

"Just do it," I yelled loud enough so she could hear. "I love you, Risse baby. But if you make me live my life without you... I'm already dead." Tears mixed with rain. My chest tightened as I awaited my sentencing, the booming click of the safety being released stealing my breath.

"PJ, stop!" Charisse screamed, closing the space between us. He stilled, dropping the hand that held my fate.

He stalked around me, coming face to face with Charisse, glaring down at her, nostrils flared, blood dripping from his nose. I looked around us. Several residents looked on, yellow lights beaming from their open windows and doors. Ms. Sonya stood on her porch, arms tight, panic riddled on her face.

"This what you want, Risse?" Spit flew from PJ's mouth, mixing with the downpour around us.

She stepped forward, her voice shaking. "PJ, you can't shoot my husband. I'll never forgive you."

PJ let out a harsh breath, shoving me before stepping back. The look in his eyes let me know this was the last time he'd ever let me off the hook. I'd tired out of warnings. His eyes, menacing black beams, only spoke of threats.

"When he fuck you over again, don't think about bringing yo' ass around here," he spat, stalking over to his mother. He brushed past her, walking into the house. Ms. Sonya ran after him, yelling curses even Satan would blush at.

Charisse turned to me, her eyes filled with something I couldn't read. "You wanna prove you love me?"

I swallowed hard, nodding. "Yeah."

"Then love me. Wholly. Fully," she whispered. "Because I can't be with a man who can't let go of his pride long enough to do right."

The fight drained out of me in an instant. "I'm sorry, baby," I whispered, cradling her face in my hands, pressing our foreheads together. "I'm so sorry, baby. Please forgive me." I kissed the wetness of her cheeks, the saltiness of her tears, bitter reminders of the pain I caused her time and time again.

This time would be different.

I'd be different.

I'd give her the world and more.

"Don't. Don't say you're sorry and keep doing the same thing," she whimpered. "My heart breaks with every promise you break," she cried.

I let out a shaky breath. "Charisse, baby, please. I can't live without you."

She didn't answer.

I brushed my nose against hers. She just stared at me as the rain kept falling, waiting for something neither of us knew how to name. I wrapped an arm around her waist and ran my free hand up and down her arm. Chill bumps rose along the trail I made as she continued to softly cry against my face, her eyes shutting tight, trying to stay strong.

I placed gentle kisses across her forehead, on the tops of her cheeks, and across her jawline. With each kiss, the guard she had up, barring me from her, relaxed. I pulled her closer, rubbing my hands across her back. Angling her face to meet mine, I kissed her lips. She opened up to me, our tongues drawing together like magnets.

We stayed like that for what felt like an eternity. Her in my arms, back where she belonged. The creaking of an opening door broke our trance.

"Bring y'all asses in this goddamn house," Ms. Sonya yelled. "I'm 'bout tired of y'all bringing y'all mess to my porch. This'll be the last time, shit!"

Charisse and I broke into laughter, smiling at each other as we entered the living room. Ms. Sonya stood in the hallway, a sad, stern expression on her face. She walked over and stood face to face with Charisse, her voice weary but firm. "I hope you know what you doing, baby girl. You cash in them wooden nickels, ain't no turning back."

Charisse trembled at my side. I squeezed her tighter in my arms, trying to warm us both. She was back. I was home, and I'd never let her go again. From this moment forward, it was until death do us part.

———◈———

Months had passed since that night in New Orleans. Charisse and I sat curled up on the couch, soft music playing in the background. Things had changed. Our love was different now. Stronger, more intentional. I wish I could say the same for her and her family.

"I talked to Mama today," she said, her fingers tracing patterns on my chest. An episode of Martin played on the TV in the background.

"And?"

She sighed. "She said PJ still doesn't want to hear your name."

I kissed her temple. "He'll get over it. I'm not going anywhere."

She shifted to look up at me, studying me a moment before nodding. "I hope you're right. I know PJ has his issues, but I still miss him." We sat in comfortable silence, watching Martin clown Pam for the umpteenth time.

"Who do you think our son will look like?" I asked simply. "Me or you?"

"Oh? So now you're ready for kids?" Charisse laughed, shaking her head. "What would everybody say?"

"I don't care what everybody has to say," I smirked, pulling her closer and straddling her thighs across my lap.

Her eyes searched mine, her fingers tightening against my shirt. "You serious?"

I nodded. "Yeah. I mean, I know things aren't perfect, but that doesn't change what I want with you."

Her gaze turned serious. "You really want this?"

"With everything in me," I responded, grabbing her hips, squeezing the soft flesh.

She leaned in, her lips brushing against mine, slow and sure. "Then show me."

And I did.

I leaned in, my lips brushing against the hollow of her throat, breathing her in, letting her feel the weight of what she was doing to me. She shifted against me, a slow, deliberate roll of her hips, her mouth hovering just above mine.

I wanted to see her like this forever. Wanting me, waiting on me, coming apart for me.

"I love being your wife, Kenneth," she whispered, freeing my dick from the shorts I wore.

I caught her mouth in mine, my hands sliding up the curve of her thighs, fingers gripping the soft flesh just enough to make her gasp into my kiss. I swallowed the sound, deepening the kiss, pulling her closer, letting her feel exactly how much she was getting to me. She moaned softly when I shifted beneath her, entering her, pressing her against me in a way that made her breath stutter.

"Damn, baby," I muttered against her lips, one hand slipping beneath the oversized t-shirt she was wearing, squeezing her breasts that fit perfectly in my hands. She moaned as she rode me, her hips rotating to a beat in her head.

That was it. That was all I had in me before I lost the little bit of control I'd been holding onto.

She shivered when my fingertips grazed the dip of her spine, her back arching instinctively, pressing her chest to mine.

I needed more. I needed her.

I tilted her head back, kissing a slow path along her jaw, then lower, my tongue tracing the spot along her collarbone that always had her melting. She whimpered, and my grip of her thighs tightened, guiding her against me, dragging out a slow, delicious friction that had us both breathing harder.

"You feel what you do to me, baby?" I whispered, my voice thick with need.

She nodded, biting her lip, her fingers sliding beneath the hem of my shirt, nails raking over my stomach just enough to make my muscles tighten.

She was teasing me. Testing me. And I was about to show her exactly why that was a dangerous game.

With one swift motion, I shifted forward, flipping us so that she was pinned between me and the couch. Her breath hitched, hands gripping my arms, but her legs stayed locked around me, like she didn't want to let go.

"You always this needy, Mrs. Reid?" I smirked against her skin, trailing kisses down her chest.

She exhaled shakily, her hips moving against mine, slower this time, deeper. She wasn't running anymore.

And I wasn't letting her go.

Vivian

"All The Man I Need" - Whitney Houston

THE COLD STERILITY OF the gynecologist's office did little to soothe the anxious energy thrumming inside of me. I sat on the padded exam table, the crinkling paper beneath me a stark contrast to the heavy silence in the air. Douglas sat beside me in the stiff chair, his fingers laced together, his brows knitted in concern.

Dr. Patel, a petite woman with sharp brown eyes and a calm demeanor, adjusted her glasses before speaking. "Vivian, after reviewing your test results and considering your medical history, I want to discuss an option that could improve your chances of conception."

I straightened, my heart pounding. "What is it?"

Dr. Patel folded her hands on the desk. "There's a medication, Clomiphene citrate, that stimulates ovulation. It's often used for women struggling with infertility."

Douglass exhaled sharply beside me. "So, it could help her get pregnant?"

"Yes," Dr. Patel said with a measured nod. "It increases the likelihood of ovulation, and in turn, conception."

Relief and hope bloomed in my chest, but Dr. Patel's tone kept me from getting ahead of myself.

"However," she continued, "there are risks and side effects we need to consider. The most common include hot flashes, mood swings, nausea, and bloating. In some cases, it can cause ovarian hyperstimulation, which can be dangerous. And because it stimulates multiple eggs, there's an increased chance of multiple pregnancies."

I barely hesitated. "I can handle all of that," I beamed, overjoyed that I could bring my child into the world.

Douglass tensed beside me. "Vivian, slow down. Let's think about this."

Dr. Patel's gaze softened as she looked at me. "One more thing, Vivian. If you do conceive, I strongly advise that you consider adjusting your workload. Stress can negatively impact any pregnancy, and given your history, a high-stress job may not be in your best interest."

"You're saying I should quit my job?" I swallowed hard. My career flashed before my eyes. All the hours I'd been putting in at the law firm, trying to make junior partner, would go down the drain.

Dr. Patel shook her head. "Not necessarily. But cutting back, reducing stressors. Those would be wise choices to give yourself the best possible chance to carry to full term."

Douglass shifted in his seat, his fingers tightening together. "Vivian, you love your job. I know how badly you want to make partner."

Determination solidified in my chest. "I want this baby more."

He exhaled, rubbing his hand down his face. "I just... I don't want you risking your health for something that's not a guarantee."

"You can't think like that, Douglass," I said, my voice steady. "I have to try. I want to be a mother. I can't just sit back and do nothing."

His eyes searched mine, filled with love, fear, and reluctance. Finally, he reached for my hand, squeezing gently. "If this is what you want, I'm with you. But we do it together, okay? No hiding how you feel, no pushing yourself too hard. The second this starts being more of a problem than the solution, we're done. You understand?"

I nodded, a lump forming in my throat. "Together."

Dr. Patel offered a small smile. "Then we'll get started on your prescription. It may take a few months to see any action, but we'll monitor it closely and adjust if needed. But for now, take time to think it through before making any final decisions."

I didn't need time.

I already knew.

This was the choice I had to make.

A month passed since I'd started taking the medication, and nothing changed. No double pink lines. No signs that my body was responding the way it should. Just hot flashes, mood swings, nausea, and an exhaustion that lingered day and night.

Every morning, I woke up hopeful as I took the medication.

Tonight, I would go to bed frustrated, disappointed.

I sat on the couch, staring at the blank TV screen, my arms folded tightly over my chest. The air in our home felt suffocating. I couldn't understand. I cut back on hours at work. Tom Peterson got the promotion instead of me. I ate every food known to promote fertility. I wasn't stressed.

Well, at least I pretended to be.

And still, none of it had worked. It was as if the universe had a mind of its own. It needed to get with the program – my program. Douglass moved around the kitchen, the sound of pots clinking together in the silence. I hadn't said much all day. I didn't have the energy.

"Vivi, dinner's almost ready," he called out. His voice was soft and careful.

I exhaled through my nose. "I'm not hungry."

I heard him sigh, and then a few moments later, the couch dipped beside me. Douglas reached for my hand, threading his fingers through mine. "I know you're tired. I know this has been a lot, but, baby, good things take time."

I swallowed hard, the pressure in my chest growing tighter. "But what if time isn't enough? What if this never happens for us?"

His grip tightened. "Then we try again. Or we can try something else. But we don't give up. And we don't let this take away from the joy we still have."

I blinked rapidly, trying to push down the tears that were threatening to spill. "I just... I thought by now, we'd be celebrating."

He cupped my cheek, gently tilting my face toward his. "The only answer that matters is that I love you. With or without a baby. No matter how long it takes. You hear me?"

A tear slid down my cheek, and he wiped it away with his thumb.

"Come on," he said, standing up and tugging me with him. "You need a reset."

I frowned. "Douglass-"

"Nope. No arguments. I ran you a bath, cooked you dinner, and I'm about to put on that new TLC album you've been talking about." He kissed the tip of my nose. "You're going to let me take care of you tonight."

A small smile broke through my exhaustion. "That so?"

He nodded, leading me down the hallway. "That's so."

The bathroom was dimly lit, candles flickering on the tiled counter. The scent of lavender filled the air, and a warm bath waited for me. Douglass kissed my forehead, his hands lingering on my waist. "Get in. Relax. Let your mind rest for a little while."

I did as he said, sinking into the warmth and letting some of the tension in my muscles melt away. He sat on the edge of the tub, his fingers tracing lazy patterns along my arm.

"This is what you deserve," he murmured. "To be taken care of, to feel good, to not carry all of this by yourself. I'll work my ass to the bone to make sure it stays like this for the rest of our life."

I closed my eyes, letting his words sink in. "I don't know what I did to deserve you."

He chuckled. "Must've done something right."

I reached for his hand, squeezing it. "Stay with me?"

His eyes darkened slightly, something deeper flickering there. "Always."

The water swayed as Douglass stepped into the tub behind me, his movements slow, controlled, like he was making sure I felt every second of this moment.

I leaned forward, giving him space as he settled in, his muscular thighs brushing against mine beneath the water. The heat wrapped around us, steam curling in the air, but all I could focus on was him.

The way the dim candlelight cast shadows along the strong lines of his jaw. The way his eyes never left me, dark, intense, unwavering, as if he could read every thought passing through my mind.

The way the water licked up his chest, beads of moisture sliding between the ridges of muscles that tightened under my gaze.

My breath hitched as he reached for me, his large hands warm and steady, guiding me into his arms.

I exhaled as my spine met the firm plane of his chest, my body melting into his. His lips grazed the shell of my ear as his arms wrapped around my waist. I reached for his hand beneath the water, threading my fingers through his, squeezing.

This was home. He was home.

His body tensed slightly behind me, his grip tightening before his lips pressed against my shoulder, lingering there like a promise. And then, his hands started moving.

Slow. Reverent.

Like he had all the time to remind me exactly who I was when I was with him.

Like he wanted to erase every ounce of stress, every worry, every burden I'd been carrying.

His fingers traced a pattern on my stomach, skimming over my ribs, dipping beneath the water, teasing the edge of my thighs.

I sucked in a breath, arching slightly as his lips dragged along my neck, heat pooling in my belly as his hands continued their slow exploration.

Douglass never rushed. He never took without giving.

His thumbs brushed over the hardened peaks of my breasts, rolling the blackberry buds between his fingers. His mouth pressed soft, wet kisses along my shoulder, across my collarbone.

"You're so beautiful, Vivi," he whispered against my skin, voice thick with something deeper than desire.

My breath stuttered as his hands slid lower, his fingers teasing between my thighs, parting me, stroking me with a patience that had my nerves thrumming with need.

I turned in his arms, the water sloshing around us, my knees straddling his thighs as I faced him, hands braced against his chest, feeling the steady beat of his heart beneath my palms. I kissed him, slow and deep, tasting the heat of red wine and devotion on his lips.

His breath hitched, his fingers digging into my hips, guiding me, aligning me, until I felt him pressing at my entrance. My body trembled as I sank onto him, the water rising with our connection, waves rippling around us. His head tilted back, a slow, low groan escaping him as I took him in, inch by inch, filling me, perfectly.

But he let me take control, let me move at my own pace, let me rock against him, each movement sending warmth spiraling through my core. We moved together, not rushed, not frantic, but deep, connected, intentional.

His mouth found mine again, his kisses drugging, intoxicating, mirroring the way our bodies met beneath the water.

I rolled my hips, slow, methodical, watching as his jaw clenched, his hands gripping tighter, his chest rising and falling in sharp, uneven breaths.

"This is what you deserve," he murmured again, tilting my chin so our eyes met. "To be worshipped."

And as his lips found mine, as our bodies moved together, as I let go of everything but the feel of him, the warmth of him, the love he wrapped around me like silk.

The water sloshed around us, a slow, rhythmic echo of what had just happened, steam still curling into the air, wrapping around our tangled bodies like a whispered secret.

I stayed pressed against Douglass's chest, my head resting in the crook of his neck, feeling the way his breath was still a little uneven, his heart still pounding beneath my palms.

Neither of us spoke at first.

There was no need.

His hands were still on me, trailing soft, absentminded circles along my back, his fingers spreading warmth wherever they touched. The once-burning ache between my thighs had eased into something softer now, something that left me feeling weightless, sated, and safe.

Completely and utterly his.

He exhaled, his lips pressing against my forehead, lingering there, as if he needed the contact as much as I did.

"You okay?" he murmured against my skin, his voice still husky.

I hummed in response, letting my fingers skim along his damp chest, tracing patterns only I could see.

"More than okay."

A deep, satisfied chuckle rumbled in his chest, vibrating through me, and his hands lay lower, smoothing over my thighs beneath the tepid water, gripping, massaging, kneading.

Like he wasn't ready to let me go just yet. Like he would never be.

I tilted my head, pressing a lazy kiss against his collarbone, letting my lips linger against the damp heat of his skin. "I think you might've ruined me."

His grip lightened just a little, his teeth grazing my earlobe before he whispered, "Good."

I smiled against his skin, sighing deeper. The water was beginning to cool, but neither of us moved.

Not yet.

There was nowhere else I'd rather be.

Lisa

"My Little Secret" - Xscape

STANDING IN THE DINING room of my apartment, I flipped through the wedding binder my mother created for the hundredth time today. The final preparations were nearly done. Only six weeks until the big day, and everything had to be perfect. She'd chosen the venue, River Oaks Country Club. She'd finalized the cocktail hour and gourmet reception dinner. I never missed another dress fitting, as she'd driven me to each one. As I looked at the countdown calendar in the front pocket of the binder, something inside my stomach twisted. An uncomfortable, unsettling feeling that rose with each passing day.

Vivian and Charisse lounged on my couch, flipping through magazines and gossiping about everything: Jodeci's new album and how they insisted I was the Regine of our friend group. If there was one thing we agreed on, it was that Tupac's dating Madonna was a publicity stunt.

"You know what I don't get?" Charisse said, stretching her legs out. "How are y'all not talking about how fine Denzel was in *Philadelphia*?" She sipped on a glass of ginger ale, popping another saltine cracker in her mouth.

"Denzel being fine is not new information," I smirked. "But nothing tops Malcolm X Denzel."

"True," Vivian laughed, propping up the magazine in her hands. "But look at this picture from his new movie coming out next year." We all glanced through the article and pictures.

"I don't know how I feel about that thin mustache," Charisse frowned, eating yet another cracker, crumbs flying as she spoke.

"Of course you wouldn't," Vivian said, rolling her eyes. "Kenneth has got to have the thickest mustache this side of the planet."

"And I love it," she shot back, rubbing her stomach. "And I love him, too." I couldn't believe Vivian and I missed the showdown that took place between Kenneth and PJ. If it weren't for the bruises and cuts on his face, I wouldn't believe it to this day.

Part of me was slightly envious of Charisse. She had a man willing to die behind her, and here I was, settling for a business arrangement.

"How are you feeling, Risse?" Vivian asked, touching Charisse's barely there bump. "You haven't stopped glowing yet," she smiled.

"Ugh. Tired. Hungry. Sleepy. Nervous." She stopped speaking for a second, pulling her lips into her mouth. She grabbed both our hands and held them on her belly. "But I'm so happy. I've never been happier." Tears sprung to her eyes, and damn it if they jump to mine and Vivian's.

"You look happy, Risse," I said, swiping one of the free-falling tears.

"And Kenneth. Oh, he's been so amazing. Never misses an appointment. When he's not at the hospital, he rushes out to get whatever craving I have." She wiped more tears from her eyes. "He swears we're having a boy, but I don't know. I think it's a girl."

Charisse and I laughed while Vivian continued to smile, but I caught it – the slight dimming in Vivian's eyes, the way her smile faltered just enough before she buried it beneath that usual poised exterior.

She was holding something in.

I knew it.

Charisse must've noticed it too, because she tilted her head, studying Vivian with concern. "Viv, are you ready to share what's been bothering you the past few months?"

Vivian hesitated, her fingers smoothing over the fabric of her skirt. Then, with a long, shuddering sigh, she leaned back into the couch.

"Douglass and I...we've been trying to have a baby for months."

The words fell into the space between us, heavy and raw, unspoken agony women into each syllable. Then, just as quickly, her face crumbled. She dropped her head into her hands, soft, heart-wrenching sobs breaking through the gaps in her fingers.

"We've tried everything, and nothing's worked."

My chest tightened at the sound of her tears.

Charisse and I shared a look before Charisse reached for her hand, holding it tight, grounding her. "It's going to happen, Viv. I know it will."

I nodded, settling on the other side of Vivian, rubbing soothing circles into her back. "You and Doug are meant to be parents."

Vivian inhaled sharply, trembling against the weight of her emotions. She lifted her head slightly, her usually sharp, composed features now vulnerable in a way I'd rarely seen before.

"I hope so."

She wiped at her face with the sleeve of her shirt, swallowing another sob, before exhaling and forcing a small, wobbly smile. "We're trying this drug to stimulate ovulation. I've been on it for two months. The doctor says it takes three to get a positive read on a test. I'll probably have to leave the firm if it works."

The words sounded mechanical, like she'd been repeating them to herself, trying to convince herself she was okay with them.

I exchanged a glance with Charisse, both of us picking up on what she wasn't saying.

"Is that something you want to do?" I asked.

Vivian's hands trembled as she grabbed a tissue from the coffee table, blowing her nose before answering. "I used to think I'd never want to be a stay-at-home mom." Her voice wavered. "My whole life, I've worked for this career. I wanted the title, the prestige, to be one of the best Black female lawyers in the game."

She exhaled sharply, her lips quivering. "But now? Now, I can't imagine a life without a mini-me or mini-Doug running around."

Her face twisted in frustration, in anger at the unfairness of it all, at the choices being forced upon her.

Charisse squeezed her hand tighter. "Motherhood won't erase this amazing person that you are. It'll only add to it," I said, stroking her cheek, swiping a few stray tears.

Charisse nodded. "And you are not alone in this. You have Douglass. You have us."

Vivian closed her eyes, another tear slipping free despite the deep breath she tried to take.

"What does Doug say?" Charisse asked, placing her ginger ale and crackers on the table.

"He just wants me to be happy," Vivian sniffled. She let out a short, breathy laugh, shaking her head. "And since these investments he's making are paying off, we'll be more than comfortable with me staying home."

"It'll happen, Viv," Charisse said, her voice more than reassurance. It was a declaration. A certainty. She pulled Vivian into a hug, her arms wrapping around her. I joined them, the three of us holding onto each other, a tangle of limbs, love, and unspoken promises.

This was sisterhood.

This was what we did – holding each other up when the weight got too heavy.

Charisse pulled back slightly, grinning through her own misty-eyed emotions. "You're getting pregnant, then it'll be Lisa, and we'll raise our kids together."

I rolled my eyes, wiping a tear from my cheek as I leaned away. "Don't spread that baby dust this way. Let me get down the aisle first."

We giggled, letting the moment become quiet, the weight of it all settling between us.

Vivian exhaled deeply, her body finally releasing the tension she'd been holding onto for too long.

We would be okay.

She would be okay.

And when the time came, when we were standing at her baby shower, rubbing her belly and listening to her complain about swollen ankles, we'd remember this moment.

The moment she didn't have to carry it alone.

Later that night, after Vivian and Charisse went home, my apartment was silent and peaceful. I poured myself a glass of wine and sat by the window, staring out at the city lights. I barely had a chance to take a sip before a knock sounded at my door. I knew who it was before I opened it.

Trent leaned against the frame, hands in his pockets, the same cocky smirk tugging at his lips, the same mischievous green eyes dancing in the dim light. "You busy?"

I gave him a look. "You're asking me that at eleven at night?"

He shrugged, stepping inside without an invitation. "Maybe I just wanted to see the future Mrs. Wright one more time before she ties herself to a life she doesn't want."

"I'm not doing this with you, Trenton." I rolled my eyes, closing and locking the door. My heart pounded in my chest. "I told you last time was the last time."

"That's what you said last time." He walked up on me, a predator toying with his dinner. I stepped back until my back hit the wall.

He lowered his face to my neck, inhaling deeply before exhaling, his warm breath circling my neck. My eyes shuddered as I willed my body not to react.

"You've got a lot of nerve, showing up here." I swallowed, my mouth dry. "Wesley could show up any minute."

"One," he started, leaving a trail of wet kisses from my ear to my collarbone. "We both know Wesley ain't popping his ass up over here. And two. I got a lot of things, including a feeling that you don't really wanna go through with this wedding."

"You're ridiculous," I panted, my palms flat on the wall behind me. Trent's hands roved up my side, his thumb brushing the underside of my breast. The touch was electrifying, making me arch into his chest.

He pulled back. "Am I?" He tilted his head, our eyes locking. "Lisa, come on. We both know the only reason you're walking down that aisle is 'cause it makes sense on paper. But love ain't about logic. It's about how a person makes you feel. And I know damn well he don't make you feel the way I do."

I swallowed hard, refusing to let his words sink in. "Even if that were true, Trent, you still haven't said the one thing that would make me call off this wedding."

Trent's smirk faltered for the first time since we'd started our little late-night rendezvous. His jaw tensed. He hesitated, the fear of saying something he couldn't take back. I looked into his eyes, the hazel-green, darkening into a stormy moss-gray.

"You can't say it, can you?" I whispered. "Because as much as you don't want me to marry him, you still won't give me the security I need."

He grabbed me by the waist, tight enough to leave traces of his fingerprints long after tonight, my body flush against his. "I can give you a lot of things, Lisa."

"But not that. Not a lifetime."

Silence stretched between us before Trent finally exhaled. "Then let me give you all of me tonight."

I didn't answer with words. I just pulled him toward me, kissing him with everything I had. Because this was it. The last time. One more night to pretend we could've had something real.

Because my choice was made.

The wedding countdown would continue, but for now, I would let myself forget.

The dining room was quiet, save for the soft clinking of silverware against fine china. The scent of buttered seafood drifted between us, but I wasn't hungry. I hadn't been since I sat down. Since I realized, once again, that this wasn't dinner. It was a final evaluation.

I adjusted my posture, folded my napkin neatly in my lap – just as my mother had taught me – and smiled as Mrs. Anna Wright recounted her latest charity gala. Across from me, Wallace Wright nodded in approval. My mother, Evelyn, sat beside me, a picture of grace and expectation.

I was used to this world, used to knowing what to say and when to say it. But I still felt like an actress playing a role in a movie that had already been written for me.

"And of course," Mrs. Wright said, beaming at me over her wine glass, "we'll expect to see you and Wesley at next year's gala as the guests of honor. A married couple is always the best representation of stability in our community."

I smiled politely, the same way I had since I was a little girl at these types of events. "Of course."

Before I could shift in my seat, I felt Wesley's hand brush against my knee beneath the table. A small touch, almost imperceptible, but grounding. He wasn't staking a claim. He wasn't trying to control me. He was just making sure I was okay.

Surprised, I turned my head slightly, glancing at him from the corner of my eye. He wasn't looking at me like I was a prize to be won, a challenge to be conquered, or an obligation to be fulfilled. He was just seeing me.

"You okay?" Wesley murmured, low enough that only I could hear.

I nodded once. He didn't press.

"I tell you," Mr. Wright said, cutting into his fish with practiced ease, "nothing gives a man focus like marriage. Wesley's been closing development deals left and right now that he's got something worth working for."

I braced myself for Wesley's usual cool, effortless response. He was good at this, at knowing exactly what to say to please his father, uphold the image. But instead, for the second time tonight, he surprised me.

He set his fork down, carefully, and shook his head. "I've always been focused, Dad. But Lisa... she's not just something I'm working for. She's going to be my partner. If anything, I'll be working even harder to be worthy of her."

His words settled into the air like something solid and real, something that didn't belong to the performance happening around us. My mother, usually so measured, studied him with renewed approval.

"And that is just the kind of husband I want for my daughter," she said, nodding. "Oh, Anna, I can't believe the wedding is just a few short weeks away," she beamed across the table. Our mothers ended the dinner discussing all the wedding plans, as our fathers discussed a few business deals.

Me, I exhaled, a breath I hadn't realized I was holding. For the first time since our engagement had been arranged, I thought maybe this wouldn't end in disaster.

Maybe I could be happy.

I turned to Wesley, finding something steady and knowing in his expression. Something that told me he understood exactly what I was thinking.

He leaned in slightly, just enough to keep his voice low. "You're thinking hard over there, Lisa. Second thoughts?"

I tilted my head, searching his face. He wasn't exciting like Trent, wasn't chaos and heat and wild temptation. But maybe that wasn't a bad thing. Maybe calm, steady, and safe was exactly what I needed.

I let the corners of my lips tilt upward. "No... Just thoughts."

"Oh really?" A hint of a smile hit his lips. "Do share. Inquiring minds would like to know."

"This entire engagement, we've only spoken in mixed company. I think it'd be nice to know something more about my future husband, outside of his current business dealings."

"So, what do you have in mind?" he asked, turning to face me, placing an arm across the back of my chair.

"Why don't we have a night cap back at my place? After dinner? Then you can tell me who Wesley Wright is, outside of the office." I sipped the remainder of my wine, letting the fruity notes linger on my tongue as I held his gaze.

He smirked and looked down, then back at me. "I think I can make that happen," he replied, biting his bottom lip.

Yeah, maybe there was more than meets the eye when it came to Wesley Wright.

Staring at my reflection in the lit mirror of the vanity, all I could focus on was the small stick tucked away in a mountain of toilet tissue at the bottom of the trash can back in my apartment. My hands trembled as I traced the edge of it, my stomach twisting in knots. The two pink lines had appeared clear as day that morning, confirming what I'd suspected. My boobs had grown larger, my nipples sensitive. Strange smells made my eyes cross.

I was pregnant.

When the two lines appeared, I felt like I couldn't breathe. I thought that on today, my wedding day, I'd just have wedding day jitters. But nothing like this. Nothing like carrying a secret so heavy, I felt it pressing and growing against my ribs.

My bridesmaids flitted around the room, excitement buzzing in their words. My mother fretted over everything: my dress, bouquet, and veil. I looked past my reflection in the mirror, all the movement in the room a blur. Mentally, I counted back the weeks, scared at what the final calculation would be.

The door creaked open, and I jumped when I saw Wesley standing there in his tux. He looked polished, composed, stable.

"Wesley," my mother shrieked. "Don't you know it's bad luck to see the bride before the wedding?"

"I don't believe in luck, Mrs. Davis." He stepped inside, closing the door behind him. "Can you ladies clear the room? I'd like to speak with my future wife."

The ladies looked at each other, then at me. I shrugged, letting out a shaky laugh. "Y'all go ahead. I'm fine." My mother and bridesmaids scurried out of the room. My mother frowned at Wesley as she passed him, her nose pointed in the air, lips pursed.

"How are you holding up?" he asked, stepping closer to me.

I stood from the vanity, smoothing my dress. "Is it that obvious?"

"A little," he smiled. He slid his hands into his pockets, tilting his head as he studied me. His amber eyes glazed over my face. His freshly lined beard looked nice against the shiny, tanned skin of his bald head. Dark, thick eyebrows added to the seriousness of his face. "You aren't having cold feet, are you?"

I swallowed hard, unsure how to respond. How was I supposed to tell the man I'd had as many conversations as the fingers on my hand, that we were having a child much sooner than we'd agreed?

He stepped closer, his voice lowering. "Lisa, I know this isn't exactly how you pictured your wedding. Hell, I know this isn't the kind of love story little girls dream about." He exhaled, shaking his head. "But I need you to know that I will do everything in my power to make sure you live a life so comfortable, Princess Di would be envious."

Something about his words, the quiet reassurance of them, made my throat tighten. It was the most romantic thing I'd ever heard him say, so far from the business lingo he normalized in all our previous conversations. And before I could stop myself, the truth slipped out. "I'm pregnant."

Silence hung heavy in the room.

Wesley blinked, then slowly nodded, his expression unreadable. "I see."

My fingers curled against the vanity. "I don't know-"

"I know," he said, cutting me off gently, understanding lacing his tone. "And we'll handle it."

"What do you mean?"

"We'll tell everyone the baby came early," he said simply, taking my hands in his. "A honeymoon baby. No one will question it."

My chest tightened. "Wesley..."

He brought my fingers to his lips, kissing each digit gently. "Lisa, I knew what this was when we agreed to our parents' wishes. I understand this marriage might never be filled with love, that it's about what makes sense. And making sense of things and this? That's what I do best."

My lips parted, but no words came out. I'd expected panic, maybe even anger. Instead, he was offering me a way out of uncertainty. A way to move forward without chaos.

A way to stability.

A soft knock at the door interrupted us. "Lisa," my mother started, ice in her voice. "We need to put the finishing touches on your dress!"

I turned to the door, seeing Vivian and Charisse peeking inside. I nodded at Wesley, who gave my hands a final squeeze before walking out, leaving me with my bridal party.

Vivian arched a brow. "You okay?" I nodded my head.

My mother passed around champagne flutes, her irritation from earlier subsiding. "Alright, ladies. Let's make one final toast to my daughter." She poured the fruity, bubbly liquid into everyone's glasses. Vivian covered her hand over the top of her flute.

"I'll have to toast with air, Mrs. Dixon." A sparkle reached her eyes.

"Viv, are you?" Charisse asked, rushing over to her, hand on her belly.

Vivian shook her head vigorously, tears sprinkling her cheeks. "It's still early. I don't want to get ahead of myself."

Charisse squeezed her hand. "It's still worth celebrating."

"Oh, another baby! How exciting!" My mother rushed to me, ready to fill my glass. "Here, Lisa. Have double to make up for Vivian."

I placed the glass on the vanity, my hands trembling. I hesitated for half a second before blurting, "I'm pregnant."

The gasp that went around the room could've been heard halfway across the world. Charisse squealed, pulling me into a hug. "Girl! Congratulations!"

"Charisse, you know this is all on you, right?" Vivian laughed, coming over to hug me. "You spoke this into existence."

"Of course I did. I knew it would happen just like this," she said, bouncing on the balls of her toes. "Our babies are going to grow up together and be best friends. Then, their babies will be best friends. I can't wait!"

"You're terrible," I groaned, burying my face in my hands. "Mama, are you going to say something?"

She stared at me, her eyes glistening with moisture. As she walked toward me, Vivian and Charisse dropped their arms, wrapping them tight around my waist. My mother grabbed my chin in both of her hands. Her mouth held a wistful smile.

"I'm so happy for you, baby. I know the circumstances weren't ideal, but I'm happy you and Wesley were able to find some love in all of this." She kissed both of my cheeks before wiping her eyes. She shook her shoulders, a wide smile covering her face. "Let's go, ladies. This baby needs their parents to tie the knot."

Just then, Wesley's mother burst into the room, a flurry of excitement filling the space. The wedding march was about to begin, and it was time to head to the altar. I took a deep breath as my mother adjusted my veil, tears shining in her eyes.

"Ready, sweet girl?" she whispered.

I glanced at Charisse and Vivian, who nodded in reassurance, then back at my mother. I squared my shoulders, inhaled deeply, and smiled.

"As ready as I'll ever be."

With that, we all filed out of the room, our dresses flowing as we made our way toward the ceremony space. The mountain of uncertainty I'd started the day with subsided as I stepped forward, one foot in front of the other, toward whatever came next.

Vivian

"Love No Limit" - Mary J. Blige

T HE ROOM WAS WARM, bathed in soft morning light filtering through the blinds. The world outside felt distant, muffled by the quiet hum of the hospital monitors. But inside this small, sacred space, everything felt perfect.

Vanessa lay against my chest, her tiny fingers curling and uncurling, already grasping at the world around her. My heart clenched as I traced a gentle finger down her round, chocolate cheek, marveling at the beauty in my arms. Her face was all mine, even though she had Douglass's warm brown skin. Her wide, brown eyes had tiny flecks of gold in them, open, observing everything once she'd come out. It took all of two seconds before we realized she had pipes of steel. Lungs that hadn't stopped showing us they knew how to work the entire time we'd been in the hospital.

"She's perfect," Douglass murmured beside me, his voice thick with emotion.

I turned to look at him, my partner in everything, his eyes softer than I'd ever seen them. "And it only took her three years and umpteen hours of labor, unmedicated, to make her arrival."

Douglass laughed, grazing a finger over our daughter's thick head of hair, the nine months of heartburn paying off. I'd never be able to eat spicy foods again. I was sure of it.

"She's going to do something great, Doug," I whispered. "I feel it. With me as her mother and with you as her father. There's no way she won't make a difference in this world."

He smiled, leaning down to press a kiss to my forehead. "She's already changed mine."

A knock at the door pulled us from our quiet bubble. Charisse strolled in, Kenneth following behind her, a six-month-old Kelly propped on his hip.

Kenneth exhaled dramatically as he took in the scene. "Man, I thought one of us was gonna have a boy. Now, who am I going to teach about having game with the ladies?"

"Shut your ass up, Kenneth!" Charisse snapped, walking over to me. "Let me see my goddaughter," she cooed, sitting on the bed next to me.

Douglass chuckled. "Guess the universe had other plans. We'll have to trade secrets over tea parties now."

"Yeah, yeah," Kenneth mumbled, shifting Kelly in his arms. "That's okay, though. My Kelly baby gonna run these negroes ragged. Watch and see." He kissed Kelly, that gorgeous little girl with the biggest smile I'd ever seen on a child, even my own.

"Well, isn't it the two fathers of the year." Another voice cut into the room.

Trent leaned against the doorway, smirking, and Kenneth rolled his eyes. "Man, look at this clown. You need to get yourself one of these."

"Yeah," Douglass laughed. "It might humble your ass."

"Oh hell nah," Trent responded, walking to the foot of my bed. "I'm just here to bask in the moment and witness the beginning of y'all's downfall. Both girls? Oh yeah, y'all about to catch hell."

Before Kenneth could throw something at him, another knock sounded, and Lisa stepped in, Wesley, now Wesley Sr., by her side, a one-month-old Wesley Jr. cradled in her arms. Lisa's eyes flickered toward Trent before quickly shifting away.

The tension was thick enough to cut through.

Wesley cleared his throat. "Congrats, you two. Vanessa's beautiful."

Douglass nodded. "Appreciate it, man."

Sensing the shift in the room, the men exchanged glances. One by one, they shuffled toward the door, making their excuses.

"Alright, we'll leave y'all to do whatever sentimental shit y'all do. Douglass, I got a cigar with your name on it," Kenneth boasted, pressing a kiss to Charisse's cheek before heading out. Trent hesitated for a split second before nodding at Lisa and walking away. Wesley lingered a moment, giving Lisa a look that she returned with barely a perceptible nod before following the others.

And then, it was just us.

Vivian, Lisa, Charisse.

Mothers.

We sat in silence for a moment, letting our new realities settle in.

"I can't believe we're actual mothers," Lisa finally said, sitting on the opposite side of Charisse. "Like, we have actual kids that depend on us now."

"Who would've thought?" I added, shaking my head. "I mean, I always knew I wanted kids, but damn, actually having them? Holding them?" I glanced down at Kelly, struggling to free herself from her mother's arms and crawl toward me.

Charisse exhaled, looking between Vanessa and Wesley Jr. "We can't mess this up."

Lisa and I nodded.

"We won't," Lisa murmured. "We're going to do right by them. Make sure they have everything they need. Make sure they never doubt how much they're loved."

Charisse smirked. "Make sure they don't make all the dumb choices we did."

That made us all laugh, even as tears shimmered in Lisa's eyes. The noise made Vanessa scrunch up her face. Not even a millisecond later, she was howling loud enough to break glass. Kelly pulled herself up my arms and sucked on Vanessa's cheek, the touch seemingly calming this howler of a child of mine. Wesley stayed quiet, tucked in the crook of Lisa's arms, looking on.

Lisa, Charisse, and I sat there, soaking it in, absorbing the unspoken vow between us.

To do better. To be better. To love our children fiercely and unconditionally.

And as I held Vanessa closer, staring into her eyes. I knew this was only the beginning.

The mistakes, the triumphs, the heartbreaks. The next generation had arrived.

And their stories were just getting started.

Looking for More?

If you made it this far, first of all — thank you. Thank you for reading, for loving these characters, and for letting my words live in your heart for a little while.

But we're not done yet.

This next story? It gets deeper. Book Two takes everything you just read — the tension, the tenderness, the unfinished business — and turns the volume all the way up.

Keep reading for a **first look** at what's coming next...

And if you want even more exclusive content (bonus scenes, behind-the-scenes breakdowns, and early access to the full book before anyone else)? Join my Patreon fam:

www.patreon.com/AlexandreaLeChelle

That's where the real magic happens.

Now, go on... turn the page.

Khalil

T HE NIGHT WAS ALIVE with the kind of energy that only Ma Josie's house could create. The walls shook from the bass of the bounce music streaming from the speakers in the living room. Old school songs by DJ Jimi and DJ Jubilee had the older crowd reliving their younger years. Laughter and clinking glasses echoed through the house as folks gathered around, either dancing, drinking, or locked into the card game happening in the dining room.

I leaned against the door frame, a glass of bourbon in my hand, my eyes scanning the room. Zay and Nessa were slow dancing in the corner, lost in their own little world as always. How they managed to slow dance to "Get It Ready, Ready" by DJ Jubilee was beyond me. Lynn and Nyah were at the table with Zay's mom and Mr. Ted, their laughter accompanying Ma Josie's curses of Mr. Ted reneging during the spades game. Nessa and Kelly's parents were doubled over in laughter at the commotion. My pops kept topping off everyone's cups, adding fuel to the fire.

But me. My attention kept drifting toward Kelly. As it had the minute she began her descent down the escalator when she and the rest of the crew arrived at the airport. Including Chris, the new dude she wasted her time with, still denying the love we had between us.

She stood across the room, her long-sleeved cropped polo showing off her svelte waist, leading to the loose jeans that hung ever so carelessly off the roundness of her hips and ass. Her longs braids, with wavy pices of hair swept across the fullness of her ass, leaving whispers of kisses across both cheeks as she moved around. I took another sip of my drink, wincing as the burn from the alcohol did little to soothe the ache in my heart.

Kelly laughed at something Chris said. A deaf man could hear the fakeness of it, the subtle bit of exasperation that made the noise sound winded toward the end. But not Chris. He didn't pay attention to the way her teeth clenched through her forced smile, the slow drag of her eyes as she sought an escape from whatever smug nonsense he was spewing. Every time he leaned close, his hand on her lower back like it deserved to be there, I laughed at the recoil of Kelly's muscles. The little tilt of her body as she tried to keep some space between them.

When was she going to be tired of fucking around with lames?

Kelly and I had been playing this dog-chase-the-cat game for years. And I fed into it every time. *Every. Single. Time.* Each time I thought we were getting somewhere, she'd pull back, blaming school or work or her desire not to be in anything serious. And each time I sat back, played my role where she saw fit for me in her life, knowing I wasn't ready for anything serious either. But seeing her with another lame ass dude, acting like he was cool, but dripping disdain with every word uttered from his mouth, tested every ounce of patience I had left.

"Yo, Khalil!" My father called from the dining room, a knowing smirk on his face. "You jumping in this next game or what? Josie looking for somebody to back her since Ted's about to get kicked out," he laughed.

"Nah, I'm good," I said, pushing off the doorframe. "I'm just vibing tonight."

Zay looked up from where he and Nessa had been glued to each other all night, raising an eyebrow in my direction. He knew me too well to believe that I was just "vibing."

As the night went on, I settled in the living room with Zay and the others, as our parents took over the dining room, their laughter and chatter barely audible over the music. Betty Wright's voice filled the living room with soulful strains of "Tonight Is the Night," her lyrics weaving through the air like smoke, sensual and full of longing.

I slouched back in the armchair, one arm slung over the back, the other holding my third double shot of bourbon since we'd been at Ma Josie's house. I swirled the glass around, the melting ice clinking against the glass as I stared across the room, getting a clear view of Kelly and Chris on the loveseat. As much as she resisted looking at me, her body language told me we were in tune. Every time I shifted in my seat, she did the same. Every shake of my head was followed by a gentle switch of her own. Every sip that met my lips was matched with a heavy gulp of her own drink.

And Chris, for his part, looked smug as ever, his arm slung across the back of the loveseat like he owned the damn thing. On the adjacent sofa, Nessa sat atop Zay's lap, her head resting on his shoulder as they laughed with Lynn and Nyah. They'd been talking about our college experiences when Betty's song about first times began playing.

"Man, y'all don't know nothing about this," Zay said, grinning as he kissed Nessa's temple.

"Please, Zay," Nessa said, rolling her eyes. "You act like you were a grown man when the song came out. You were even a thought."

"Ay, but when I did hear it, I knew it was going to be a classic," Zay shot back.

"It was already a classic," Lynn laughed. "How are you going to decide what something is after it's already been decided?"

Zay smirked. "'Cause I did, that's how."

"Alright then, Mr. Know-It-All," Kelly said, smirking. "Since you know so much, why don't you tell the room about your first time? That's if you're not too shame."

I leaned forward, laughing inside when Kelly did the same. "Yeah, my boy. Go on ahead and tell everybody about it. We won't laugh."

Zay laughed, shaking his head. "Y'all nosy as hell."

"That's still not a no," Nyah said, angling her head around Lynn. "Come on, don't leave us hanging.

Zay looked at me, amused. "Aight, aight," he said, holding up his hands. "but only becuase I know Khalil ain't gonna share shit. My first time was—"

"Awkward," Vanessa interrupted, laughing. "Just know, by the time he met me, he knew where all the pieces fit." Nessa gave Zay a kiss on the nose, then glared around the room, threatening anyone to say something.

The room erupted in laughter, everyone except for Kelly and me. Chris, now picking up on the tension, grew quiet. I took a slow sip of my drink, daring him to say something to me with my eyes.

"What about you, Kelly?" Chris asked, his eyes never leaving mine, his voice a knife cutting through the laughter.

Kelly blinked, her smile faltering. "What about me?"

"Your first time," he said, his tone pointed as he turned to face her. "I bet it's a good story."

Kelly's lips pressed into a thin line. "I don't kiss and tell."

"Really," Chris asked, his eyes narrowing, then throwing a quick look in my direction. "I find that hard to believe."

"Say Chris," I bellowed, not liking what he tried insinuating about the woman that had my entire heart to do with as she pleased. "Slow your roll. She said she don't kiss and tell."

"Why?" Chris asked, sizing me up. "Got something to hide? I don't understand why you care anyway."

The once playful mood in the room vanished. Nyah, Lynn, Nessa, and Zay looked back and forth between Chris and me.

"I ain't got shit to hide," I said, downing the remainder of the bourdon in my hand. "And I care because I was there."

Kelly's head snapped toward me, her eyes wide. "Khalil—"

"And if I remember correctly, it was a damn good time, right Kelly?"

The room fell silent, save for the music playing from the speakers and our parents cutting up in the dining room. The revelation I'd just made crashed around the living room like a wave.

"Kelly, what the fuck is he saying?" Chris questioned, his nostrils flaring.

Kelly stood abruptly, her cheeks flushed with a mix of anger and annoyance. "Excuse us, she said tightly, grabbing Chris's hand and pulling him toward the front porch.

I watched them go, my jaw clenched, the air in the room still humming with the aftershock of my words. I set my glass on the coffee table, a bit harder than necessary. Ma Josie was going to cuss my ass out if I scratched her antique table. I leaned back in the chair, my eyes fixed on the door, a hard stream of air escaping my lungs.

"Khalil," Nessa started. "You did not have to go there."

"Well, what you expected me to do? Old dude wanted to know, so I told him. Weren't y'all the ones asking about people's first times?"

The others deadpanned in my direction. "Khalil," Nyah started. "We all know about you and Kelly. She told us as soon as she came back home."

"Yeah, do you really think we'd keep something like that from each other after all these years?" Lynn questioned.

I shrugged their comments off, focusing instead on the sliver of porch I could see from the window. Chris moved closer to Kelly's face, telling her something that made her expression shift. My fist clenched as he leaned in closer, getting in her face. Kelly moved back a bit, her hands going to her hips in the way she did when she was getting ready to tell somebody off. She'd done the same movement for as long as I could remember.

I stood, pulling up my pants as I moved to the front door. I saw Zay move Nessa off his lap as he rushed to meet up with me.

"Ay, don't do nothing stupid. We grown now and this my mama house?" he warned.

"Come on now, you know me better than that. I'm just making sure she good."

Xavier rested a hand on my shoulder. "You sure that's a good idea? I ain't trying to have you boxing dude on the yard."

"Says the guy who was ready to slide Wesley's face across the conference table last year." That comment brought out laughter from the women still sitting on the couch.

"Yeah, baby. I still don't know how you jumped to those conclusions. He's so clearly into—Ouch!" Vanessa squealed as Lynn pinched her thigh.

I chuckled as I walked out the door.

Kelly

PLAYLIST: "Love Galore (feat. Travis Scott)" -
SZA

WHEN I STEPPED OUTSIDE, the cool night air hit my skin like a shock, a welcome break from the suffocating tension filling the living room after Khalil opened his big mouth. Chris followed me out, his steps heavy with whatever attitude he was carrying. I don't know why he was so upset. We weren't even that serious for him to act like his feelings were hurt about something that happened a little over ten years ago.

I crossed my arms, turning to face Chris as we reached the edge of the porch. "What's your fucking problem, Chris?"

"My problem?" he whined. "You bring me out here to spend time with you and your family, and you do everything but pay attention to me."

"What do you mean, pay attention to you. This trip is not about you."

"I don't understand you. All this—" he gestured back to the house, the music, the commotion spilling out from inside. "This isn't who you are. It's an act. Where are we anyway? Is this the projects?"

Heat rose to my face, as my chest tightened. I laughed from deep within. How he figured we were in the projects while being nestled in the heart of Gentilly was troubling?

This is the dude you picked.

"An act?" I started, my voice rising. "This is exactly who I am, Chris. This is part of me. My grandmother's house was two streets over. These are my people. You don't get to stand here and tell me otherwise."

He stepped closer to my face, his voice low, arms crossed over his chest. "Please, Kelly. This whole 'hood girl' thing might work with your little friends, but we both know the truth. For godsake, you're about to be a board-certified pediatrician. Act like it."

The words hit like a slap, but I refused to let it show. Why was it so difficult for people to see I was more than my upbringing, my education, my career? Just because I grew up in a world of private schools and debutante balls, didn't mean I loathed the summers spent eating kool-aid pickles and nachos from the snowball stand.

"Ghetto?" I said, backing up an inch, ready for Chris to get out of my space. "Let me tell your stuck-up ass something. Don't you ever fix your mouth to talk down on me like I owe you an explanation for who I am."

"Kelly—" he started, but before he could finish, the front door opened, creaking into the night air.

The humming in my veins let me know who it was before he crossed the threshold.

"Y'all good out here?" Khalil's voice was low and dangerous, stirring up something deep within me.

Chris turned, startled, but quickly recovered. "This doesn't concern you, Khalil."

"Oh, see that's where you fucked up. Everything about her concerns me, ya dig," Khalil said, stepping closer. "And what you not about to do is stand here and disrespect her like that. I don't give a fuck what y'all got going on."

I felt my stomach twitch, desire flaring hot and fast, with a little mix of anger. "First of all," I said, turning to Khalil. "I don't need anybody defending me, especially not you, Khalil. I can handle myself."

"I know you do," he said, his eyes laser-focused on Chris. "But that don't mean I'm about to let this dude talk to you crazy."

Chris scoffed, crossing his arms. "I can't believe you're slumming it up with his kind, Kelly. It's pathetic."

Khalil's jaw tightened, his shoulders squaring. I needed to end this conversation before someone left in an ambulance. I was 1,000% sure Chris would end up pressing charges.

"Nah, the only thing pathetic around here is you. You don't know the first thing about Kelly, and honestly, you don't deserve to be standing here talking to her. Why yo' wack ass here anyway? Kelly, send your man's packing."

"So you listen to him, huh?" Chris accused, arching his brow.

"I don't listen to anybody but myself. I tried to wait until we were back in Houston, but I can't. I think it's best you leave in the morning.

Chris' face hardened, his pride clearly stung. "For the record, I don't need some girl who's confused about who she is standing beside me."

"Confused?" I repeated, my voice cutting through the cool air like a blade. I stepped forward, tilting my head, letting out a sharp laugh. "Boy, let me make one thing fucking clear. The only thing I'm confused about is how I let you think you had a shot in the first place."

Chris blinked, but I wasn't done. I planted my hands on my hips, giving him the full weight of my glare. I could feel Khalil's grin behind me, urging me on. "You want someone 'suited' to be on your arm? Good luck, because you couldn't handle a woman like me, even on your best day. You'd fold the second I let you taste this pussy."

I leaned in just slightly, my tone dropping to a lethal edge. "Instead of worrying about finding somebody good enough for you, worry about that little dick problem you got. Plastic surgeons work miracles. Ask my dad for a reference since you been up his ass this entire trip."

Chris muttered something under his breath as he walked back into the house, but I didn't care. The sound of the front door shutting was all the closure I needed. I stepped aside, starting to head in the same direction, but Khali's voice stopped me.

"Remind me to never get on your bad side, Lily-girl," he smiled, clearly thinking my anger was meant solely for Chris.

"Shut the fuck up, Khalil. Go find somebody else to play with instead of worrying about what I have going on."

He stepped closer to me, breaking the bubble of space I typically kept others out of. I took a shallow breath, his cologne overpowering my senses, trying to break down my defenses.

"Why you pissed off at me?" He spoke lowly, the rumble in his voice matching the beating of my heart, trying to still my nerves. "Ain't nobody told you to bring that pretty ass boy out here. I bet he packed more clothes than you."

"You don't get to do that," I shot back, staring into his golden honey eyes. *Snap out of it, Kelly.* "Why is it every time I have something going on, you do what's ever in your power to come between it? Do you see me interfering with all the girls you bring around?"

"It's 'cause you know it's nothing to interfere with. All you got to do is say the word, you know I'm kicking them to the curb." He grabbed me by the wrist, brushing his lips against the delicate skin. I closed my eyes, taking in a deep breath. "Besides, I can't help saving you from yourself."

"I don't need you saving me, Khalil. I'm not your mother." His lips stilled on my wrist as his eyes darkened. He dropped my hand, standing taller than he was, his presence looming over me on the barely lit porch.

"Let that be the last time you bring up my mama." He moved past to enter the house first. He looked back, shaking his head. "And stop settling for bum ass niggas, just becuase you afraid of something real."

I didn't respond. I couldn't respond. I so desperately wanted to say something, anything, when a small smirk tugged at the corners of Khalil's lips, knowing he'd taken back the upper hand. I entered the house as he held the door open for me, pushing aside the confrontation, choosing instead to focus on what was happening in front of me. My parents getting along, my friends having the time of their lives in a place that held so many memories for me.

Whatever this thing was between Khalil and me, it wasn't over. Not by a long shot. But for now, I needed to let it simmer on the back burner until I was ready to face all that came with it.

About the author

Born and raised in Houston, Texas, with roots stretching across Louisiana, Alexandrea has always felt a deep connection to the stories of the South. Having lived in both Texas and Louisiana all their life, she noticed a gap in literature representing the real, complex issues faced by people in these regions —particularly within the Black community. This gap sparked their journey as a writer.

Inspired by a desire to bring untold stories to life, Alexandrea writes with the purpose of shedding light on critical topics like gentrification, mental health in the Black community, parental wounds, and the importance of creating safe spaces for Black women and men to express their emotions. But above all, her work emphasizes the beauty of healthy Black love and the power of Black women being cherished and celebrated.

An avid reader, bullet journaler, crafter, and cook, Alexandrea finds creative fuel in everyday activities and in the work of influential authors like Toni Morrison, Zora Neale Hurston, Kennedy Ryan, Sadeqa Johnson. Many of the themes explored in her debut and future novels are drawn from personal experiences or those of close friends and family, making each story a deeply personal and authentic reflection of life.

What began as a hobby during a winter break from teaching quickly evolved into a passion that brought her newfound purpose. Through their writing, Alexandrea hopes to offer readers not only an escape but also a deeper understanding of the challenges and triumphs within the Black community. For anyone aspiring to write, her advice is simple: "Just start. There is someone out there who needs to hear your story."

Also by

The Double Back Diaries:

Loved By You (Book #1)

The Choices We Make (Novella #1)

Lily In The Valley (Book #2, Coming Late 2025)

9 798991 816335